CHANGES
True Horror Hides
In The Smallest Happening...

Edited by Dorothy Davies

CHANGES
**True Horror Hides
In The Smallest Happening...**

GRAVESTONE PRESS

Table Of Contents

Deadly Threshold

Marise Morland

26.10.62

"All this will soon be gone," Lynn said mournfully.

"It won't happen," said Ross with all the authority of his sixteen years. "There won't be a nuclear war. Kennedy and Khruschev will back down."

"I didn't mean them. I meant – this." She drew an arc in the air.

They were sitting on the remains of a wall, overlooking a wilderness which had once been carefully tended flowerbeds. Some stubborn perennials still flourished amid weeds, grasses and nettles. Close by, a sycamore and lilac bush vied for supremacy. Further off, fronting the main road, stood four empty houses, awaiting demolition.

In the centre of the right-hand plot were two scattered heaps of gravel and sand. Old Mr. Cubbage in the end house had been about to lay a path when the compulsory purchase order arrived. He'd downed tools in anger and never set foot in the garden again. Two doors along, a patterned vase stood proudly in an empty bedroom window, its faded gilt paint catching the rays of the setting sun. This, the last owner had explained, was to signify that her home was still loved and would be, until the last brick fell.

"Alice's café will be next," Lynn continued. "Then the pub and our street. We'll probably be sent to opposite ends of Wycombe."

"I'll visit you."

"No you won't. You'll be working in London. With computers."

"I never mentioned London."

"It stands to reason. There aren't any computers round here."

"Oh, I think there are one or two," murmured Ross, raising his eyes to the opposite hilltop.

From the valley, little could be seen of the USAF base save for two masts, black against the evening sky, a baleful red light atop each one. Lynn glared at them.

"It won't happen," Ross repeated. Then, apparently changing the subject: "Have you heard of the Many Worlds Interpretation?"

"Is that more of your science fiction?"

"No, a scientific theory. There could be many realities similar to this one, occupying the same time and space. We'd never see them, of course."

"And your point is…?"

"That there might be another Wycombe where old Fred got to finish his path and Mrs. Denney and her vases didn't part company. The council will have given everyone grants to get their roofs repaired, instead of demolishing whole streets."

Lynn was silent for a time. "Then why aren't we in *that* version?"

"Maybe we're in both. Maybe *you're* the computer expert and I'm... whatever you decide to be. Had any more thoughts on that?"

"Not yet. Ask me next week – if we're still here."

"Ross! Dinner!" called his mother, three doors away.

Lynn remained where she was after he left, watching the rooks settle in the stand of oaks to the west. It had been such a beautiful autumn. Still was. Suddenly, distantly, she heard music; Brian Hyland's "Sealed with a Kiss." It seemed to come from the direction of Alice Heydon's café, which was puzzling. Alice had a battered old radio permanently tuned to the Home Service. When Lynn pushed branches aside for a closer look, the light streaming from the open back door was neon white, not the usual uncertain yellow.

Lynn took a few more steps forward and paused, astonished. The tired interior of the café was gone and in its place was a traditional American diner: chequered floor, bar stools, shiny chrome fixtures and a Wurlitzer. Everything looked brand new. Had Alice sold her business? Who'd have bought the café when the entire row was due to come down? More to the point, how had the new venue been installed with no sounds of building work?

The room had one occupant, a girl of around Lynn's age, blonde hair tied high in bunches. She wore a pink and white candy-striped dress with a flared skirt and plain pink bodice embellished with seed pearls. "I opened the door and here you are!"

she said, somewhat obscurely. "I'm Sadie. Sadie Nevins." She had a warm, confiding American accent which didn't match her faintly aloof gaze.

"I'm Lynn Taylor."

"I know. I've seen you outside with your boyfriend. Ross, I believe."

"He's my neighbour," Lynn said defensively.

"Boyfriend," Sadie insisted. "And he's cute. You should bring him with you next time."

Lynn ignored this. "Is this diner for US personnel?"

"Well, natch."

"Then where are they?"

Sadie looked away. "The base is on alert. Cuba."

"But you still have permission to be out?"

"If my dad says it's OK, then it's OK. He's Lieutenant General Ira Nevins, in charge of Pine Tree Base."

"Pine Tree? It hasn't been called that since the war."

"There's always a war somewhere," Sadie said airily. "Let's have some more music. Can you do the Loco-Motion?"

"No."

"Then c'mon, I'll show you." She pressed keys on the juke box and proceeded to chug around the empty tables. "See? It's easy. Do you like my dress? It's from Saks. My mom sent it over. She's still in New York – my folks are divorced. But hey, we've got Saks catalogues at the base so why don't I bring you one? If you see anything you like I'll say it's for me and get Mom to send it."

"Oh, I'm not sure…" began Lynn, bemused by Sadie's rapid-fire chatter.

"Listen, I've just had a great idea. We could do one of those – what are they called – cultural exchanges. You could go see New York and I could stay with *your* mom."

This was getting alarming.

"I'm in my last year at school," Lynn improvised. "I've got exams, important ones. Maybe once I've left…"

"I'd really like that," Sadie went on as if she hadn't heard. "Your little street, your gardens, they're so – English!"

"I have to go," Lynn said firmly. "It's my dinnertime."

"But you'll come again tomorrow," persisted Sadie. "Bring Ross."

"I'll mention it to him," Lynn said neutrally and stepped out of the door. The music stopped abruptly. Once she'd regained the lane, she looked back. There was no neon light, only the tangle of trees and what appeared in the twilight to be the outline of Alice's café.

27.10.62

She did go back, of course. Ross's grandmother's car was outside his house, which meant he was at home for the day. Lynn didn't see Sadie as a rival – Ross was unimpressed by spoilt rich girls – but she didn't want him to think she was making fun of his many worlds theory. So, before she even mentioned the diner, she needed proof it

11

existed. Something small, like a matchbook or beer mat.

Once inside, however, she had other concerns.

"The base is in lockdown," Sadie announced. "The missile crisis. We're at Defcon 3."

Lynn wasn't sure what that meant, but it sounded ominous. Sadie was staring out of the front window, so she went to see what was holding her attention. She expected to see only the Rye Park, the river and a few dog-walkers. Instead, the park was full of servicemen – running, standing in groups, driving Jeeps across the grass.

"If there's a lockdown," she said slowly, "why aren't they back on the base?"

"They *are* on the base," Sadie replied, as if talking to a slow-witted child.

Lynn looked again. A lorry, which had been obscuring the park entrance, pulled away to reveal a barrier, a checkpoint and an armed detail. She now knew with absolute certainty that this was not *her* 1962.

Someone else had entered the diner: a gaunt, weary man in a creased uniform. "You shouldn't be here," he said. He wasn't looking at Lynn.

"Sergeant Edsel," said Sadie. Her voice dripped disdain. "Always the party-pooper."

"You really shouldn't be here," he repeated.

"Butt out," Sadie advised.

"I'd better go," Lynn said, flustered. "I don't want to cause trouble…" She backed away, leaving Sadie and Edsel bickering with each other. A few random phrases reached her:

" – not my fault she wouldn't tell him. I tried."

12

"I don't care about that any more. This just isn't right."

She managed to grab a coffee spoon on the way out. There was a sudden influx of air as she crossed the threshold, reminding her of the updrafts in the London Underground. Later, when she searched, the spoon was no longer in her pocket.

Back at the diner, the argument continued. Sadie had shed the posture and speech patterns of a sixteen year old and now looked several years older. "You're such a wimp. I thought you were with me on this."

"At first, but not now. You're a piece of work, Sadie. You'd walk all over anyone to get your own way."

She didn't deny it. "CalTech sent Schehedrin's latest figures over. He calculates the portal won't exist after tomorrow."

"Defectors will say anything."

"The math checks out."

"And you're the expert, are you? Maybe it's all bullshit. Why aren't CalTech's slide-rule guys all over this?"

"You've seen the evidence. You've seen the girl."

"I've seen your useless attempts to follow her."

"Schehedrin explained all that. The balance has to be kept. There has to be an exchange of mass. Mine for hers."

Edsel sighed gustily. "And how do you know she'll be back?"

"She will be, you'll see. This continues tomorrow, with or without you. In the meantime

13

I'm going back to HQ to lose this stupid goddamn dress!"

28.10.62

"Lynn! Lynn, have you heard?" Ross bounded up to her as she was heading for their meeting place. "It's over! Khruschev made a broadcast this morning. He's moving the missiles."

"I heard," Lynn said, forcing a smile. "You were right. It was just sabre-rattling. So now I can go back to worrying about my career."

"I can only stay a minute or two," Ross apologised. "I promised Barry I'd help mend his tape recorder. Again. But if I finish in time I'll look for you."

"Fine. It's all fine," Lynn said. She'd just caught a glimpse of neon through the trees.

"What are you staring at over there?" Ross asked teasingly. "What's so interesting about Alice's back yard?"

He can't see it, Lynn thought. Why can't he...?

He ruffled her hair. "You're really grounded in this place, aren't you? Every twig, every leaf. I'll see you later. Be good!"

Right, thought Lynn. One more visit. If I don't get a souvenir, he'll never believe me. Now the panic's over, there might be some actual customers in the diner. I might even get a cup of coffee!

But there was only Sadie and Sergeant Edsel, both at the far window.

"We're at Defcon 1," said Sadie without turning round.

Lynn hardly dared look. The park was full of randomly running figures. The brutal shape of a military helicopter hovered close by. Sirens began to wail. And above the ever-familiar treeline rose a pall of black smoke shot through with flame.

"It's the missile silos," Sadie said emotionlessly. "Sabotage. We can't launch."

"You put missiles *here?*"

"Inside the hill. Perfect for them. Grab her, Bill."

Lynn's arms were pinned behind her back.

"It wasn't your boyfriend I wanted, you silly little girl," Sadie continued. "It was your *life.*"

"You still can't get out," Edsel reminded her.

"Because I've nothing connecting me to her space? You're wrong. I do." Sadie held up two sycamore seeds. "These were stuck to her jacket the first time I brought her through." She took a few steps toward the portal. "Bye-by, Lynn. Enjoy the rest of your life. All four minutes of it!"

Suddenly the grip on her arms loosened.

"Run!" yelled Edsel, giving her a shove toward the back door and freedom.

Lynn ran.

Sadie screeched and clawed at Edsel as he hauled her back from the threshold. "Sorry, sweetheart, you don't get to do this," he declared.

Lynn tumbled outside, tried to run, tripped on a tree root and fell sprawling. The updraft was stronger this time, wrenching half-dead leaves from the bushes, picking up twigs and soil and small pebbles and rolling them past her. She clung to the root, afraid to get up or even look up.

15

Ross, returning in search of her, halted at the diner for the first and only time. Dimly, as if through layers of semi-opaque glass, he saw Sadie, beating her fists on an invisible barrier. "Let me through!"

As he watched, her flesh began to glow with white radiance, dazzling in spite of the darkness closing over the portal. The light consumed her until only her skeleton was left, until it too burned away, leaving only a skull which bared its teeth in one last vengeful snarl: "Let... me... through!"

Then there was nothing but the late afternoon sun, glancing off the thinning sycamore and burnishing the vase in Mrs. Denney's window.

"What did you see?" Lynn whispered.

"Tell you later."

"She's gone, hasn't she? Sadie? In the other reality?"

"It's *all* gone. Come on, we shouldn't hang about." Ross helped her up and put an arm round her as they walked. Soon, they'd share what they'd seen of the militarised, possibly doomed town. And they'd also agree never to tell anyone else . Except, perhaps, in the guise of fiction.

They descended to Easton Street, re-acquainting themselves with its shabby normality. Alice's café was closed, of course, but she'd be there early tomorrow, cooking her greasy breakfasts. The park was just a park, with its river and rowing boats and children's playground. At the entrance was the derelict flour mill, its water wheel stilled, its walls covered in posters for local events. And further down the road was the dairy shop run

16

by Kit Smith, whose tabby tom habitually slept on a sack of dog biscuits and bit anyone who tried to move him.

"I've made my career choice," Lynn suddenly announced. "I want to be an archivist. These streets, the houses, the people who lived in them – they'll all be forgotten unless someone keeps records. I can do that."

"Even if it means learning Latin?"

"I can do that too. The past informs the future, Ross. Someone has to keep it safe."

"Yeah," he said softly. "Someone does."

***

Years later, a developer and his investor stood in the wasteland where Lynn's street had been. They didn't know it, but they were in the exact spot where Fred Cubbage had dumped the materials for his path.

"I think you've made a good choice," said Bryce, the money man. "This is a prime site. Are the plans ready?"

"Tomorrow. Forty luxury flats and thirty town houses."

"Any planning issues that you know of?"

"None. It'll be a pushover. Now are we done here?"

"Hold on." Bryce scuffed at something with his boot, then used his handkerchief to pick up a piece of green glass. "This is very odd."

"What's odd about a broken bottle?"

"This isn't glass. It's fused green sand. Trinitite. Anyone been letting off nukes around here?"

"Of course not!"

"I'm not kidding, Sam. I've toured the site in New Mexico where they tested the first A-bomb. It's a museum now. This stuff was lying around everywhere, but we weren't allowed to take any. They said it didn't exist anywhere else."

"Then how did this piece get here?"

"No idea. Mischief? A competitor?"

"Should we report it?"

"Are you nuts? We can't say anything. The Contaminated Land geeks would descend on this place and - end of the project. We wouldn't get permission to build for twenty, maybe thirty years." He dropped the piece of trinitite and scooped earth over it. "There. Hopefully it'll disappear once excavations start. You OK with that?"

In the pause that followed, the merest whisper of a song reached them. "Yes it's gonna be a cold, lonely summer…."

"Someone's car radio," Bryce said eventually.

"Must have been."

They left, walking a little too quickly.

Life Changes

Dorothy Davies

The parking meter said there was still one hour of parking time left.

The shame was the driver had gone, taking their ticket with them. One hour wasted. But the parking space was available, can't have everything in this life. Slide the car into the slot, pay for a ticket, drop it on the dash for the ever intrusive traffic wardens to see, lock the door and go.

To what?

Why had he asked for the meeting? And in such a public place? Franco's, for goodness' sake! Packed to the doors usually with avid diners, as in avid eaters and listeners. It did not bode well for the future of our relationship.

He'd said in his voicemail, 'don't book longer than an hour; no need to give them money unnecessarily.' But dinner at Franco's took two hours, start to finish, lingering over liquors afterwards and all.

To what? The question came up again in my mind.

The end, of course. Why else invite me to a one hour meeting in our favourite restaurant where we always spend two hours... why speculate? Heels clicking, I headed for Franco's, trying to quell the butterflies and sickness churning in my stomach.

Whoever said there was such a thing as heartache was wrong. It's stomach ache - every time.

Cold, bitterly cold. The wind played with litter, tossing it here and there, occasionally getting bored and throwing a hat into the game instead until it was rescued by its irate owner. Boot heels thudded on the chilled pavement, eyes seeking the warmth were attracted by steamed up windows which said, 'in here is hot, hot, hot!' but they weren't Franco's and the man I loved would not be there, waiting.

My fingertips began to ache with the cold. Come on; hurry, would that I could have found a parking place nearer!

At last, the door opened into warmth, rich smells of good food and richer coffee, ears assaulted with clink of cutlery on china and the rolling massed sound of voices.

He sat alone at a table for two, frowning. I knew that frown so well: it boded ill for the meeting.

I waved, he looked up and smiled. Franco's waiter took my coat; I made my way through the furniture to the chair opposite him and sat down.

'What...'

His gesture said silence. The waiter came back; I ordered a starter and a large coffee. I saw he had nothing in front of him. The water went away without asking what he wanted. The cold which I had walked in had come in to the restaurant with me; it sat low and angry and grew infinitesimally as we looked at one another across the clarity of the white tablecloth.

'Don't be angry.' His voice was low, laden with unbearable sadness and then I knew. Knew with absolute certainty that our time together was done.

The coffee came, steaming, tempting, cream floating swirling on the top, even as my emotions were swirling as I tried to come to terms with the ending of something wonderful.

'How long have you known about this?'

'Ah, you would ask that, my loved one. Three days. I've been thinking on our past for three days and cried a million tears. I'm all cried out.' But he wasn't, a stray tear was creeping down his face and he dashed it away with a hand that was quickly restored out of sight under the table.

Not before I saw it. The hair was long, dark and thick.

It had begun.

It was over.

I drank the coffee, holding the cup in both hands, staring into the darkness of its depths. He said nothing, waited as I thought about everything and absorbed it.

'It's been good.'

'I hoped you'd say that.'

'It's been more than good, it's been wonderful. I'll be a long time finding another like you.'

He laughed, gently. 'I hope not exactly like me, or you'll have to go through this again.'

'If all of your type are like you, then I would face it and handle it and love him as I've loved you.'

'Thank you.' Another tear. It had been an outrageous lie that they were done.

I had no tears. They would come later.

'Now I understand why you told me only to pay for an hour. You've shut down, you're not eating and I couldn't sit here and eat a meal while you had nothing.'

'Precisely.'

The cold had gone. In its place was aching grief, loss and pending loneliness. A different feeling entirely. Why had I been so certain he was dumping me? Foolish, foolish person that I am. I should have known his love was greater than that.

I didn't expect this so soon. He said we had some years ahead of us. Maybe he miscalculated. I dared not ask.

'How much...'

'A lot. This is the last time I can come out in public.'

The starter came, I prodded at it, ate a few mouthfuls, pushed it away. It was good but my appetite had gone.

'Your hour is going fast.'

'It means nothing if this is our last hour together.'

'I would not have you leave knowing there was a parking ticket waiting for you!'

The laugh I loved, low, sexy and inviting, was still there. Everything was still there, it was just that it would be smothered under layers of thick dark hair very soon, the face would change, a muzzle would form, the arms would change and lengthen, the spine curve, a long tail would emerge and the man I loved would become a wolf. A werewolf.

I knew that werewolves could be human for a long, long time, changing now and then but that the time would come when the change was permanent. He had told me, freely so I knew what I was getting into, that this was his last time. When he changed back, he would not be able to be human again.

I thought I could handle it.

I found I couldn't.

I had dreaded this day from the moment we fell in love. Now it was here.

I got up, fumbled for money but he pushed it away. 'My treat. Go enjoy your life. It's been – wonderful. Better than any before. Hold on to that.'

I nodded and walked over to the door. The waiter handed me my coat, sympathy radiating out of him. He knew. Somehow he knew and he hadn't questioned anything. I thanked him as best I could and hurried out into the coldness.

The wind brought tears to my eyes; it was the wind, yes?

But not enough tears that I couldn't see the parking ticket stuck on my windscreen when I got there. I had gone over the hour after all.

Just as I had gone over the time with the werewolf who had stolen my heart.

Unless I could find another – and what were the chances of that happening? I was going to be lonely for a very long time.

The trouble was; I needed to find another. Who else understood the need to take time out every full moon and hide? The other problem was; I had a long way to go before I could change back and stay that way forever.

I knew when I did, I'd seek him out and we would be together for eternity.

Before then there was a life to lead. It did not involve paying for time.

I tore off the parking ticket and went to find the traffic warden. It was close enough to full moon for me to have begun the change.

Some people should be careful whose car they target...

Sing a Dry Song

Rickey Rivers Jr

In the town square the mayor stood near the podium. An emergency meeting had been called. The townsfolk gathered in groups, some whispering before the proceedings began. Everyone had questions.

"Morning," said the mayor.

"Morning," said the townsfolk.

The mayor sucked his teeth. "Look ya'll, there's some serious matters we have to discuss this evening."

There were murmurs.

"Aw, don't be glum. It's just the ole mayor asking simple questions, as I tend to do. Ya'll know me."

Some of the townsfolk smiled.

"Now look here, we all know what must happen every year. Our little town gets a wee bit smaller. We all know and understand this, correct?"

"Correct!" said everyone.

"Glad we know that. Now, since we know what matters need to be done to ensure a blessing upon our humble town, why then, pray tell, would someone sully the lamb?"

There were whispers now. People started looking at each other, confused.

The mayor shook his head. "I ain't accusing nobody of nothing. I just want to ask a simple question aloud. Did anyone have anything to do with the lamb being sullied?"

There was no answer. A young girl raised her hand. "What you mean by sullied?"

"Well," said the mayor, finding the words, "I'll be frank with ya'll and I know there's no frank in town." He laughed, pulling his suspenders. "The sacrifice, as we know him, was found with blood and residue dripping out of him."

The townsfolk grumbled. Whispers became louder. Someone was laughing.

"This ain't a laughing matter," said the mayor. "I'm serious when I say that this person must atone. A person can't sully the lamb. How else can we show thankfulness? If the lamb is sullied we'll be cursed, surely. We can't survive winter much less the rest of the year. If anyone knows anything, speak now."

The crowd was silent. There was head shaking, awkward looks, scratching and blinks of confusion.

"Come on, ya'll. The perpetrator won't be punished; we just need to know who did it. Now we can rule out the women and children, but surely one of you men wants to confess?"

The townsmen, each with their families near, looked around and at each other. Joe Bob glared at Timothy and Timothy glared at Wilmer, Wilmer glared at Calvin and so forth. Each man was glared at by the families of each other man.

On stage the town doctor, Doctor Forest, was glaring down at every soul. He and the mayor had previously discussed the incident. Doctor Forest made the discovery and had cleaned the lamb of residue.

"Now this is ridiculous," said the mayor. "Ain't no need for shyness. We just need answers. Ya'll know how things work. If anyone needs to relieve themselves, then pigs and sheep can be provided. There's more animals here than people! We got horses too."

"Maybe one of them did it?" said a voice from the crowd. Someone giggled.

"Who said that?" the mayor scanned over the townsfolk. They all glared back.

A boy raised his hand. "It makes sense don't it? Animals get lonely too."

Again the crowd murmured. The mayor stepped away from the podium and spoke to Doctor Forest. The doctor shook his head.

"Nonsense," said the mayor. "All the animals were locked up. Whose boy is this?"

"He be mine," said Marty, grabbing the boy by the nape of his neck.

"Well. learn him some sense," said the mayor. "These matters are serious. Someone, anyone, please step forward."

The townsfolk were still. Everyone went through loud thoughts in his or her head. But no one said anything like no one knew anything. Every face was the face of a new-born.

"Fine," said the mayor, "meeting adjourned!"

And the townsfolk left slow like they wanted more, like cows unsure of a threat. The mayor put his hands on hips and shook his head. For the first time he was disappointed with them.

On the outskirts of the town was the lamb. He was naked with both arms tied to separate poles in the ground. His head was down. He was praying. The sun soaked his back. In its brilliant light he seemed to glow.

When the sun set it became dark and the lamb hummed a simple song. Soon up the hill came the mayor. He was carrying a pail of water. The mayor tilted the pail and gave the lamb a sip.

"Don't spill now. It's a long way down."

Once done the lamb nodded and the mayor took a step back.

"Look at you. I'm sorry what happened, truly I am."

The lamb moaned.

"I know. I know it was painful. But none of them said nothing."

The lamb nodded.

The mayor scratched his belly and took a step forward. He placed a hand on the boy's neck. "Nobody deserves that. Don't blame yourself."

The lamb laid rest his head on the mayor's shoulder.

"You can cry," said the mayor. "It's good to cry."

Tears came from the lamb and the mayor closed his eyes and prayed for the boy. "We all know what we've done. You're not evil for being here. The person who did you wrong, they deserve this spot. They deserve to be taken."

The lamb moaned.

"I want you to take solace in this: I believe your pain will cease. I believe your taking to be merciful. Please know that we thank you for your giving. Your soul will rain down on our town. And when you get where you're going I want you to know that me, Doctor Forest and Sheriff Carter will try our best to find the perpetrator."

The lamb shook his head and blinked six or seven times.

"It's okay, son."

The lamb made noise and shook his head more.

"Don't worry too much."

The lamb reared his head back and bellowed angry almost words.

"Calm down, boy. It's alright."

With tears the lamb moaned and mouthed something only he knew. And the mayor stood staring. The boy dangled without strength to shake the poles he used to carry to and from the farm.

"Boy, I wish you could talk." The mayor wiped his brow. "Probably shoulda kept your tongue in."

The mayor headed down the hill and back into town. He hummed a song to himself. The lamb hung his head and prayed once more. His tears fell to the grass below. His arms ached. Above the grass he saw his legless shadow and turned away. He gave attention to the sky. Dark clouds were there. Soon there was rain. And the sacrificial poles were barren.

Back in town the mayor kept the lamb in his prayers. As the townsfolk gathered all the rain they could.

"One more year," said the mayor. "Let it be done."

And children ran by with pails.

30

The Service Call

Edward Ahern

"Welcome to Do Over. *We reset you.*"

"I just killed my wife."

"That's what we're here for, sir. My name is Pradeep. First, your name, member number and password please."

Bryce had already taken the card out of his wallet. "Bryce Keeler, 47A23C2N, put upon."

"Thank you. Yes, sir, I have your informations here. I notice that you currently have our basic membership, I'd like to tell you about the benefits of our advanced 'No Regrets' level—"

Bryce felt himself shaking. "No, stop! I got a real problem here. And speak more clearly please. I'm having a hard time understanding you."

"No problem, sir, I am trained to clearly speak. But please to tell me of your problem."

Bryce keyed the video on his phone and pointed it at Dora, who lay belly down across a coffee table. The slug had torn a large hole in her back and blood dripped down from the table top, staining a white carpet.

"I couldn't take it anymore. It was her screaming at me again, ripping me up. But I only meant to scare her. The gun just fired. It's been almost five minutes now. I only have ten minutes more to reset things on my Orange watch and bring her back."

"Yes, that appears exceedingly messy. And you are so correct, sir. The Orange can only reverse your prior fifteen minutes. But you still have plenty of time. Just please to be pushing the reset button."

"No! No! I already did that. Nothing happened. Help!"

"Ah, sir, please to turn off the watch, wait five seconds and turn it back on."

Bryce's voice got shriller. "I already did that, twice! It didn't work."

The cell phone went silent for several seconds. "Mr. Keeler, would it be permissible to call you Bryce?"

"Yes, Yes, damn it, what can I do?"

"Ah, Mr. Bryce, I am not receiving a signal from your watch. It would appear to not be functional. I have attempted to restart it from here but without success. It would appear that you do not have recourse."

"But it's an Orange watch, it's guaranteed!"

"Let me please recheck. But Mr. Bryce, sir, have you perhaps poked or prodded her to ensure that she is not still living?"

"God help me! She's got a hole right through her and her stomach is all over the wall. Don't ask foolish questions. Oh hell, sorry."

"Not to be sorry. Mr. Bryce, we understand these little moments of life stress."

Bryce paced back and forth, skirting the parts of the floor splattered with blood. "You have to help me!"

"Ah, Mr. Bryce. Sir. You should perhaps have taken the 'No Regrets' option when you subscribed.

I see that the limited warranty on your basic membership expired as of last month. Unfortunately, we at Do Over are no longer responsible for watch replacement, or for indemnifying your acts of carnage. You may wish to dial 911 when we are finished.

"Or, should you go into hiding, we can offer you a reduced rate on a new and much improved watch."

"Jesus, you can't leave me like this! There must be something, some way to get my wife back. Please, you have to help me."

There was another several seconds of silence on the phone. "I have just turned off my recorder. There is a remedy I have seen on Youtube. But it is highly irregular."

"What? I'll do anything."

"Do Over does not approve of this procedure and I will deny that it was ever suggested."

"Please!"

"To remove your watch and place it in your microwave."

"What?"

"Remove the watch, Mr. Bryce, place it in your microwave and set the timer for fifteen seconds on high."

"What?"

"The watch may explode, in which case we are not responsible for damage to your microwave. If it does not explode, you have thirty seconds to remove the watch, place it again on your wrist and to touch the reset button. There is a slight chance you will be electrocuted, but then that may be your outcome in any case."

"And that will bring me back in time?"

"Nothing is certain in this life, Mr. Bryce, but I certainly hope so for your sake. Oh, and if you are able to reset, please remove immediately the watch. It is known to violently explode fifteen minutes later, causing accidental death. Good luck. I am erasing your call, there is no record of it."

The phone went dead. Bryce held it to his ear for another two seconds; then ran to the microwave and tossed his watch in. He set time and power, begged for mercy and pushed start. Sparks crackled, but the watch held together.

Bryce pulled the Orange out, strapped it on and screamed when the back seared his skin. Ignoring the pain, he ran back into the living room and punched reset...

And he was reaching into an end table drawer to take out his gun, while Dora was screaming at him. "You worthless turd, why don't you die so I can move on! And what are you going to do with that gun, you ball-less coward?"

He shut the drawer without touching the gun and turned to her. Dora kept screaming. Bryce knew he had to do something, but he didn't want to go to jail. When Dora paused for breath he said, "You're right, Dora, I'm sorry."

The words had choked him, but he continued. "We were so good together, let's try and start over. Look, I'll make a peace offering."

He unstrapped the Orange. "Take my watch, please. You've always wanted to try it. I promise you'll have a unique experience."

Mini-Mart

Thomas M. Malafarina

"There. See the sign, Vic? It says there's something called a Mondo-Mart at the next exit. Sounds like a mini-mart to me." Heidi looked out of the window with anticipation.

Victor said, "I've never heard of Mondo-Mart. What if it's a dive? As you know very well, my dear wife, not all mini-marts are created equal. Some are awesome and others are just plain awful."

"Very true. But good or bad, any of those places have everything we need. We can gas up the car, use the restroom and pick up drinks and a snack," Heidi said.

"But maybe if we hold out for a few more miles, we'll find a Swifty Mart. They're our favorite. You say that all the time. You love their iced lattes."

"Of course I do, but you know I limit myself to one per day and I already had mine at the Swifty before we left this morning. So, I don't care which mini-mart we stop at. We've been driving for hours and I not only need to stretch my legs, but I need some serious quality time with porcelain. Do I make myself clear?"

Victor laughed, "Ok, no problemo my queen, your throne awaits just off this exit at whatever the heck Mondo Mart has to offer." He put on his right turn signal and took the exit to the mini-mart.

The place was more impressive than Victor had anticipated, it had a modern brick, glass and metal facade and a stylized MM on the peaked front elevation.

"Hm… looks pretty good so far," Vic said.

Heidi agreed, "It certainly does. I wonder why we've never run into one of these before in our travels. Maybe it's a local franchise and they haven't made inroads into Pennsylvania yet."

"That's possible. If it's half as nice inside as it looks on the outside, this place might give Swifty Mart a run for their money. Come on, let's go in."

They were pleasantly surprised by the brightness and modern decor of the place. The couple traveled a lot, taking as many vacations as their schedules would permit. The result was, they had involuntarily become mini-mart aficionados. They knew what they liked and what they didn't like. They could evaluate a convenience store's potential or lack of it within seconds.

This place checked all the boxes on their list. It was clean, the smells of food were mouth-watering and had a functionally designed layout and pleasantly decorated interior. Bright lights illuminated the store, perhaps more than any marts they had ever seen. A staff of ten employees, clad in white Mondo Mart dress shirts, were busy performing their various duties around the store. There was a bank of ten computer touch screen monitors for ordering food and drinks. They could see four employees busy back in the food preparation area.

The couple agreed to answer the call of nature before picking out drinks and snacks and then they'd head out to the gas pumps to refill their tank. They walked to the back of the store, where overhead signage directed them to the restroom area and they each headed for their respective comfort facilities.

"I'll wait for you out here when I'm finished," Vic said. When he thought about it, he supposed it seemed unnecessary to say since he always waited for her in the area near the restrooms. On those rare occasions when Heidi finished first, she would wait for Vic in the same place. Although the couple had never encountered any trouble during their travels, they understood in the world such as it was, one could never be too careful, especially when traveling in an unfamiliar area.

Vic entered the men's room, noticing it was every bit as bright and clean as the rest of the store. He finished his business and went to the sink to wash his hands and looked at himself in the large wall mirror. A wave of something akin to vertigo suddenly passed over him, followed by a wave of nausea. For a moment he thought he might have to vomit. Then the feeling passed. He splashed a bit of refreshing cold water on his face and walked out of the men's room. He noticed Heidi had not yet finished her business, as was usual. He passed the time checking various things on his cell phone. After a few minutes, Vic realized it seemed to be taking Heidi longer than was typical. He hoped she hadn't become sick as he had or perhaps had another problem. Vic did tend to be the worrywart of the family and usually jumped to the completely wrong conclusion. He sighed and decided to wait another minute before sending Heidi a text to check on her.

That was when he heard his phone chimed. He looked down at his screen and saw words that simultaneously confused him and sent chills down his spine. Heidi's message read, "Where are you? Is everything ok?"

He typed a reply, "I'm standing right outside the ladies' room, waiting for you."

The response came quickly, "Stop kidding around, Vic. I'm standing right outside the men's room and you aren't standing next to me."

He typed, "Wait a second until I check something out."

Vic went back into the restroom and although bright and spacious, the door he came in was the only door available. He had been in large bathrooms with multiple entrances and exits before and wondered if perhaps he had gotten confused and went out the wrong door. He left the restroom as he had previously, but Heidi was still not waiting for him outside.

"The men's room only has one exit and I'm standing in front of it. Is it possible the ladies' room had two and you went out the wrong one?"

"Leave me to check."

He heard the phone beep and saw, "Nope. I just went back in and checked; one way in and out."

Vic thought for a moment, then texted, "Do me a favor and call my cell. If we can text, we should be able to talk. Right?"

After what seemed an excruciating amount of time, his cell phone beeped, displaying the following message, "I tried to call, but your phone just rang and rang. It didn't go to voicemail or anything. I'm starting to get freaked out, Vic. What's going on?"

"I don't know, Sweetie. I'm sure we can figure this out. Let's think about this logically. Look at the wall next to the ladies' room door. There's an employee of the month poster. Who does it say is the employee of the month?"

"Um, it says Brendan Charles is the April employee of the month."

Vic asked, "Are you sure? Mine says that someone named Zander Wells is the employee of the month."

"For what month?"

"For March," Vic replied.

Heidi said, "A month behind me. And we're at the beginning of May, so April's employee should be listed."

"What does that mean, Heidi?"

"I don't know, Vic. I'm just trying to make some observations. You know, trying to figure all this out."

There were a few seconds of no communication, then Heidi texted, "Are you still there?"

Vic replied, "Yep. One of the store workers came by and gave me the once over. I suspect he may think I'm trolling the ladies' room or something. He probably assumes I'm a pervert or something. His badge said his name was Melvin. Wow, that's an unusual name."

"Did you say, Melvin? What did he look like?"

"Skinny white kid with longish red hair and a soul patch on his chin."

"OMG. you're not going to believe this."

"Believe what?"

"I'm looking at some sort of memorial plaque for someone named Melvin Robertson. It has his picture, which fits your description. It says he died in a car accident in March."

"What are you suggesting? Are you saying somehow I've been transported to last month and this Melvin guy is alive now but won't be in a month?"

I don't know what I'm saying. I have no idea what's going on."

There were no words for a moment, then Vic typed, "Ask someone there about what happened to Melvin."

"Don't you think we should be worried about us right now?"

"Yes. But just humor me for a minute."

A few seconds passed, then Heidi texted back, "They said he died on his way home from work on March 13th. A drunk driver hit his motorcycle."

Vic replied, "Hold on. I'll get back to you."

He looked around the store and saw a cash register receipt lying on the floor. He saw it was dated March 13th. He glanced up and saw the young man, Melvin, heading for the front door with his motorcycle helmet under his arm. His shift was over and he was heading home. Vic realized he had to stop him.

"Hey, Melvin!"

He stopped and looked back at Vic, a bit confused. "Yes, sir? Can I help you?"

"Um… ah..," Vic stammered, trying to think what to say. He figured he only needed to delay the boy for a few minutes. It might allow enough time to pass so Melvin could avoid the fatal encounter with the drunk driver.

"Hey, you're that guy that was hanging out at the ladies' room. What's your deal, man?"

"Not to worry. I'm just waiting for my wife to come out."

"Oh. So, what can I do for you then?" Melvin asked, still perplexed.

Vic said, "You don't have to do anything for me. I just wanted to stop you and tell you what a nice place you have and what a great job you and your co-workers are doing. The store looks terrific. Hell, you should be the employee of the month."

"Thanks, man, but no thanks. That spot is reserved for the brownnosers. Not my scene. Look, dude, thanks, but I gotta roll."

Vic backed away, realizing that even though he had no idea how he had ended up in this bizarre situation, there was an excellent chance he had just saved this young man's life. He turned and walked back to the restroom area.

He texted, "You still there, Babe?"

"I'm here. What happened?"

"I'll tell you later. I have an idea. Maybe if we both go back into the restrooms and try to retrace our steps at the same time, we can reverse whatever it is that happened to us."

"Do you think that will work?"

"Beats me, but it's worth a try. Count to five, then walk into the restroom. Count to twenty, then come back out."

Not waiting for a reply, both Vic and Heidi counted to five then entered their respective restrooms. Vic walked immediately over to the mirror and began counting to twenty. Once again, the feeling of vertigo swept over him, as did nausea. He gripped the top of the vanity to keep himself from collapsing. When he reached twenty, he turned and walked on wobbly legs out of the bathroom.

"Thank God, you're back!" Heidi shouted as she ran over and wrapped her arms around Vic's neck. Customers in the store stared at them strangely, perhaps wondering why the woman was so excited that her husband had returned from the restroom.

"I have no idea what happened to us, but I'm so glad it's all over," Vic said, still a bit wobbly on his feet.

"Are you ok, Vic?"

"Yeah, I am now," Then he recounted his strange experience at the bathroom mirror and how he felt it a second time on his return. "This may sound strange, Babe, but I believe I was somehow sent back in time on purpose... to help that boy Melvin. And I think I might have saved his life."

"Maybe you did," Heidi said, smiling as she grabbed Vic's hand and led him over to the place where the memorial plaque had hung. "If you did, then the plaque should be gone ...."

But the plaque wasn't gone. It was still there, just as Heidi had seen it previously.

"I... I don't understand," Vic said, "If I went back to save the boy, then he didn't die and this plaque should be gone, right?"

Just then a woman with a Mondo Mart name tag reading, "Emma, Assistant Manager" came over to them.

"I see you're reading about Melvin. That was so sad and so tragic. To have been struck down at such a young age and by a drunk driver no less. Such a waste."

Vic couldn't speak, so Heidi said, "It's too bad someone couldn't do something to prevent it."

Emma said, "Yes, we often say the same thing. Just a matter of a few minutes in time could have made all the difference. On the day of Melvin's accident, one of our workers saw a man stopping Melvin at the door to compliment him on how nice our store looked. If Melvin hadn't stopped to talk to that man, he might be alive today."

All and One

Rickey Rivers Jr

This is Captain Bo Carver of the U.S. space program. I am sanctioned in the Captain's Quarters aboard the U.S. Lark V. Currently I am headed home from a routine drop off to the planet Mars beginning on January 8th. The drop off went well and all supplies are sorted. However, I regret to inform you of trouble. The trouble is I'm not alone. You'll know this once you've intercepted the Lark V. You'll also know of another change: the ship itself. We've been expanding since the drop off.

I must stress the following, which you already know: this began as a solo mission. This is now not the case. The ship is now populated. I'm one man among many. Conversations are happening in almost every sector of the U.S. Lark V. These conversations haven't stopped since their beginning. Furthermore, every day the ship grows, every day another room, every day another voice, then a voice to match that one.

In short, I'm populating an ever expanding ship. Kind enough, there are bathrooms to accommodate, beds too. Even the ship's map has updated itself to match the expansion. I won't be coy, I'm afraid.

I thought perhaps my own mind had somehow influenced the seemingly organic structuring yet I have never once dreamt of an armory existing. But there is an armory now. Why would I need one? Why anything else?

The idea of emotional construction hasn't escaped me either. However, I am not bound to the ship's mainframe and had no need to use an onboard help bot. Again, I ask why? I don't know what oddities I've come across in my travels, but they've led me here. And here now seems to be an echoing hell.

There's food of course, but only for so long. There was enough to last for the trip going and back. I'm afraid I won't actually make it. There's dozens of conversations happening simultaneously. I ask you, what happens when the food runs out? And how big can the ship become?

***

Have you ever heard a voice reverberated, your own voice speaking at the same time, conversations created and combusting? It's like living in your own skull. I'm afraid and I must return to Earth. But I fear my own return. I fear what fraction of me is actually Bo Carver in the Captain's Quarters.

I know who I am. I also know who I see, what I've seen: a bunch of Captain Bo's talking to each other and acting out their little lives as if they own them. And maybe they do! Maybe they've taken that from me? Maybe they're only molecules escaping from sweat and body waste? Maybe they'll die once we break the stratosphere? I don't know. I'm spit balling. What else can I do?

***

If you're wondering about contact with the control room or anyone within the program on Earth: communications are shot. We went through some heavy space traffic about halfway from the destination, a bunch of folks travel this time of year.

I wish I was traveling like I use to do with Cheryl and the boys. They wanted to go so many places and I wanted to take them. I intended to. I miss them.

One more thing, despite what I've said about the trip to Mars, I want to clarify that the people of Mars are not to blame. As far as I know they've not done anything but be kind and welcoming. Do not blame them for the misadventure. They are an innocent people.

This letter will travel to Earth by a titanium mail pod. By my calculations it should reach you a week before the ship's arrival. I hope you won't be alarmed seeing the ship approach headquarters. Trust and know that this is the same ship with an Earth man aboard. You will find me in the Captain's Quarters. I'm the only me in a room alone, the only me you should keep alive. It's been an honor to serve this country.

Sincerely,

Captain Bo Carver
U.S. Space Program
Transport

Mother's Child

Diane Arrelle

Regan woke up screaming.

Again.

The hands: grabbing her, holding her down, forcing her to lie on the cold metal table, pushing her feet into the stirrups, quickly faded back into her subconscious.

Faded back into hiding.

"The dream again?" Tim asked wrapping his big, beefy arms around her.

She nodded, knowing he'd understand her motion without seeing her. She snuggled against his chest and wept. She couldn't help wondering how she had married such a wonderful, caring man. A man who knew about her past and didn't care, a man who loved her for what she was, not what she had been. A man who held onto her now and was rubbing her head like a small child's and cooing soft nothings into her ear.

She struggled to get control and finally said, "Do you think it means anything?"

She asked that question after every nightmare. In the beginning she asked out of fear that there was some meaning to this recurring horror, that it was a memory and not a hidden fear. Now she asked out of habit, looking for Tim's comforting reassurances that it was nothing but a bad dream.

"You know it doesn't, it's just a nightmare," he said and kissed her. "Now, check on Marie and go back to sleep."

She nodded again and crawled from the warm bed. She smiled at her husband's big form, like a mountain silhouetted against the night sky. "I love you," she mouthed silently and started to leave the room. At the doorway she was stopped for a moment as he called, "I love you, too."

She never understood how he could do that, know her every move whether he saw it or not, but each time he reacted to her, she fell in love a little bit more.

She looked in on her seven-year-old daughter and knew she was the luckiest woman in the world. She sat on the edge of her child's bed and softly rubbed her back, feeling her even breaths. She fingered the little girl's long, unruly curls and thought about how much she adored this small, almost perfect person. Even with the uncanny resemblance to Regan's own mother, she was still able to love Marie.

She shuddered and knew it wasn't from the cold. It was the thought of her mother bringing on chills. If she never saw that woman again she would have no regrets, at least not any more than she already had and Tim was always reminding her to forget her past. She could hear his gentle voice whispering, "The past is over but remember it made you the person I love. No matter how bad it seemed to you, it is in your past and can't return."

She smiled and lightly kissed her daughter's head, then got up and tiptoed into her own bed.

After a few worried moments, she fell into a deep dreamless sleep that lasted until the alarm roused them.

Marie came bouncing into the bedroom as Regan struggled to open her eyes. "Mommy, Daddy!"

Regan sat up and smiled, "Good morning, sweetheart. How are you this morning?"

"Oh fine, Mommy. I had the neatest dream last night. It was the same one I had before. Want to hear about it?"

Regan felt like frowning but forced herself to look earnest and interested. "Go ahead," she said and wondered why her daughter suffered from recurring dreams as well.

Marie didn't seem to be suffering; she enjoyed the regularity of them. "Anyway, I'm a grown-up and I get to do all the grown-up things. I drink coffee all day long, wear lots and lots of make-up and my hair in a funny twisted bun and I smoke cigarettes..."

Regan knew the dream almost as well as her daughter, the child had told her about it so many times. She always described a typical morning of getting ready to go to work, of being someone familiar to Regan, but out of the reach of memory.

"And I have a little girl who is being bad; very, very bad. So bad that I have to work to make her righteous... I have to beat the fear of God into her because she is the child spawned of Satan--"

"What did you say?" Regan practically shouted, interrupting the narration. Marie's story had taken a turn that she never spoke of before. "A child?"

Marie blinked at her mother and then said, "Huh? What do you mean, a child?"

Regan was sweating, she could feel it on her forehead. "You were telling me about your dream daughter."

Marie laughed, "Oh Mommy, you weren't listening again. I never dreamed about being a Mommy. I dreamed about being a grown-up lady, only I won't smoke because that's bad. What should I wear to school today? Is it warm?"

Regan glanced out the window through habit and noticed frost on the roofs. ""No, it's cold so wear jeans and a sweater." She was sweating more, the beads forming over her lip tasting salty. What did it all mean? She knew Marie had just told her about a daughter spawned by the devil... she had heard it, hadn't she? Hadn't she? And not for the first time, because she'd heard it before, in her own dreams.

***

A few nights later, Regan found herself in the midst of yet another nightmare. The hands that grabbed, strapped her down like an animal, violated her in ways she didn't understand were accompanied by a voice, hated and hateful, a voice full of vile, tainted righteousness. "Do it right this time.."

Regan woke screaming!

Tim reached over and took her into his arms. "It's all right, Honey. It's all right."

Regan began to cry, heaving sobs that shook the two of them. "N... n... o!" she managed to sputter. "No, it's not!"

Tim hugged her tighter. She felt his heartbeat, steady like a life-giving machine, as unwavering as his love for both her and her child, and she calmed a little, counting the beats.

"Tim, it's not just a dream, it's something more. I know it."

"Memories?" he asked.

"I think so," she said. "I was so messed up back then, the drugs... the men... the hate."

"Forget it all," he said. "That was all a long time ago. Look at the good that came out of that time, like the you I love now and Marie. Marie came from that time; you may not know who her father was, but it doesn't matter. So, forget your fears and forget that self-hate."

"I don't hate myself anymore and with you around I'll never have to again. But the hate in this dream wasn't all mine. It was directed at me!"

The discussion was cut short by soft sobs coming from Marie's room. Both of them jumped out of bed and rushed to her room. Regan rushed over to the sleeping child and bundled her into her arms. "Wake up, Marie. Wake up; it's only a bad dream."

She saw her child open her eyes and fear shot through her like a surge of electricity. The eyes that met hers were cold and old. The childlike innocence and devotion she usually saw there was replaced by loathing. A loathing so familiar that she pushed her daughter away from her.

"Typical, Regan!" an almost adult voice shouted from the little girl mouth. "You can't push me out of your life any more than I can get rid of you. You're a worthless little bitch, a useless slut!"

Before she could stop herself, Regan's hand lashed out and slapped the child across the face. Then she quickly held up her hands to ward off any blows coming her way. Instead of being hit back, Regan heard her daughter cry out. She put down her defensive position and saw the one thing more precious than anything else in the world looking at her with a wounded expression.

"Why did you hit me, Mommy?" Marie said through her tears. "Don't you love me?"

Regan grabbed her daughter and clutched the child like a lifeline. She wept. "Oh Sweetheart, I'm sorry... so sorry. I'll never hit you again! It was because of your bad dream."

Marie looked confused. "Bad dream? I was having my good dream, the one where I'm a grown-up lady with the bad, bad, little girl who follows the pathways of Hell."

"Marie!" Regan gasped. "Stop that talk. Stop cursing!"

Regan edged off her daughter's bed and backed toward the door. "I want you to go to sleep now and I don't want to hear any more talk of bad children and bad words."

She ran to her bed, leaving Tim to tuck Marie in. She wanted to get as far from her child as possible at that moment. *What was happening*, she wondered in panic. *What was happening to her precious baby?*

Tim came in a moment later and studied her. "I guess all kids pick up cursing at school and I agree first grade is a little early, but don't you think you are over-reacting here? I've never seen you hit her before and I don't really think it was warranted."

Regan felt tears on her cheeks again and she was getting lightheaded. "Oh, Tim, it wasn't the cursing. It was... it was my mother!"

Tim came over to her and sat beside her on the bed. He put his arm around her shoulders and pulled her toward him. "Now that is someone you never mention. She's dead, why bring her up now."

Regan looked down. "She's not dead," she whispered head bowed. "I only wished her dead. I decided her dead, but she's still alive and living a few towns over."

She felt Tim stiffen and wondered if he were starting to hate her, too. This night could be the undoing of her life, she decided.

"Oh," he said, and she felt him relax. "I can understand why you feel that way after everything you've told me. The woman beat you, blamed you for everything that went wrong with her life. She was no mother; she was a waking nightmare that you had to live with for too long. I never questioned your reasons for anything you've done, but why are you bringing her up now?"

"Tim... Tim... I saw her tonight."

He looked concerned, "Where?"

"You going to think I'm crazy, but in Marie. Those eyes, that tone and those words. That wasn't my baby sitting there tonight. That was Beverly, my mother, sitting there.   A child version of the

54

bitterest, most hateful, vicious woman that ever lived.

"Regan, that's crazy."

"I know, but it's true just the same. You saw her. You heard her. Marie wouldn't talk like that, even if she picked up cursing at school, she's too young to know how to use those words and besides she spoke exactly like my mother used to talk to me. Hateful, blaming, damning."

Tim shrugged. "I think you're over-reacting. Why would our little girl take after a woman she never met? That's preposterous. And coming to her through dreams, that's even sillier. Honey, Marie is just a child exercising her new vocabulary. Let's just approach it like it is. If we explain that she's doing something inappropriate, she'll stop. You'll see."

"I hope you're right, but Tim, I'm scared. Scared for my baby and scared for myself. What if she never leaves me alone? What if she's dead and haunting me through Marie?"

Tim kissed her, made her lay down and said, "Shhh, stop worrying. We're going to prove you wrong."

"How?" she asked, too tense to relax.

"Simple," he answered. "We're going to visit your mother and sort this out. Just because you've told me Marie is the spitting image of your mother doesn't mean she has magical powers. I bet she's just a sad, old woman who'd give the world to see her daughter and meet her granddaughter."

Regan shook her head weakly, wondering if what he said could be true. "I hope you're right but

I doubt it very, very much. Beverly Todd is incapable of love or regret. And I don't want to see her ever again."

Tim reached out and took her hand. "Who is being the inflexible and intolerant one now?"

Regan didn't answer. She only squeezed his hand, then rolled over and quietly spent the rest of the night awake and frightened.

***

They were nearing the street Regan called home for the first fifteen years of her life and had an anxiety attack. "Pull over," she gasped. "I... I can't br... breathe."

Tim parked and made her get out and sit on the curb. She breathed into a paper bag for a few minutes. "Better now?"

She gave him a weak, shaky smile and knew by the worried look on his face that she had to be very pale. She hadn't slept a wink in two days, not since he told her that she was going to have to face that woman again. And now they were only a block away.

"Let's walk." She stood up on quivery legs. She felt worse the nearer they got and she needed Tim's support to make it up the five steps to the Todd's front porch.

Before she could knock on the forbidding dark brown door, it opened.

Regan took an involuntary step backwards and raised her hands to her mouth. Her mother hadn't changed at all, still tall, thin, gray-haired and

56

pinched. Her face still looked like she was perpetually sucking a lemon and the lines around her eyes and mouth were as severe as ever.

"Regan," she said in a curt, no nonsense voice. "I thought we agreed to never see each other again until I deemed it necessary. I did not call for you."

Tim stepped in from of his wife and stuck out his hand, "Hi, I'm Tim Higgins, Regan's husband."

"So?" Beverly Todd said in iced tones. "I can't help that. You bought used goods, you can't return them."

Tim frowned and opened his mouth, but Regan spoke up. "I have some questions that only you can answer."

For the first time in just about forever, Regan saw her mother smile. And it scared her. A lot.

"I'm very sure you do, after all you have all those years of drug abuse and an illegitimate child. I'm sure you have lots of questions."

She stopped blocking the door. Regan, Tim and Marie entered. Nothing had changed inside either.

Beverly motioned to the sofa and sat stiff backed on the matching chair. "So this is my, ah, my grand child? My, she really is beautiful."

Regan felt a grim smile turn the corners of her mouth down. *I just bet you would find your little look-alike beautiful.* "Yes, this is Marie. Marie, say hello to your grandmother, Sweetheart."

Marie smiled and Regan felt sure that if Beverly were at all human she would have to thaw. Beverly nodded and turned to Regan. "I presume you have finally come to your senses and are here to take me up on my offer."

Regan stared at her, opened mouth. "You've got to be kidding?"

"Why else would you come and bother me? I told you seven years ago that I would take your little bastard and raise it the correct way. So, I assume that is what is happening. That Marie has finally come to live with me."

Regan laughed. It was an ugly, barking sound, but she didn't care. "You... you hateful, old bitch. You actually think I'd give you this wonderful child to twist and ruin? You actually think after the hell you put me through that I'd let you destroy my daughter?"

Beverly stared at Regan and Regan knew if looks could kill, Marie would be motherless. "I did the best I could with you Regan. I tried to raise you righteously despite your poisonous conception." Beverly turned to Tim and explained like a teacher to a class, "Regan is a child of rape, she is the spawn of a demon and needed an upbringing that would purify her. But the taint was too deep and she proved unsalvageable, as I'm sure you already know."

Regan saw Tim getting red-faced and stood up quickly. "We'll be going now, but I have a question."

"Yes?" Beverly said with ice in her voice.

"How are you reaching out to my child? How are you affecting her over all these miles? I know she's never seen you, or met you before. Why does she have those dreams? Why is she so like you in so many ways?"

Beverly laughed.

58

Regan couldn't stop herself, she shuddered at the sound.

"Do you really want to know?" Beverly said, "Yes, I'll tell you. Perhaps you'll give me the girl then. Regan, Marie is the perfect child. I have no psychic influence over her. You see, she is me. We share our soul!"

Regan stared at her mother like she was a madwoman. "What on earth are you talking about?"

"Why, cloning, of course, Marie is my clone. I'd read about cloning in the papers. After some research, I found a biochemist who wanted funding and a guinea pig. I supplied both, I spent almost everything I owned on this, but I knew it was my moral obligation. I realized you had such an imperfect soul, such a sinful one and I knew I owed the world a replacement. What better soul than my own?"

"You really are a madwoman!" Regan said, awe creeping into her voice.

Beverly continued as if no one had spoken. "I was worried at first about sharing myself, my essence, but obviously I was strong enough to be shared. After much thought and prayer, I decided you were the perfect vessel to nurture this being, this gift to mankind. You, the actual tainted creature from a demon would nurture this angel I was making. I hoped that perhaps by carrying the new me, you could redeem yourself in Heaven. But now, after seeing you again, I doubt it."

Regan collapsed onto the sofa; her knees too weak to hold her up. Tim grabbed for her but she brushed his hand away. "No... No... It can't be! My dream was real, my nightmares were true, you drugged me and implanted me with your …your seed. Oh my God!"

Regan was screaming, tears pouring down her face. "No... no..." She jumped up and ran from the house. She didn't know how long she ran but stabbing pains in her side slowed her to a staggering walk. Her daughter, the baby she loved more than life itself, was in all actuality the one person she hated more than life itself. How was she ever going to face Marie again? How was she ever going to hug her daughter, love her child? How could Beverly be so evil?

A car pulled up alongside her. She looked up and saw Tim and Marie. "Come on in, Honey." he called. "We need to talk."

"Mommy?" Marie yelled. "Mommy why is everybody mad?"

Regan looked at the car and its passengers. She was cold and so very tired but she couldn't force herself to get in. She couldn't get near Marie.

Tim got out and walked over to her. "Come on, it's better this way. At least we know the truth now. Truth we can live with. Doubt is the killer. Come on, we're going to face this together."

Regan looked at Tim and then at Marie. "How can I love her ever again? How can I love someone I've hated for so long?" she whispered.

Tim grabbed her shoulders. "Look at me, Regan," he commanded. "She is Marie Todd Higgins. She is not Beverly and I don't believe they really share that withered soul. Marie may have inherited a little of that witch, but we can undo her influence. Come on, get in the car. Together, you, I and Marie, are going to prove that environment can defeat heredity."

Regan stood frozen. She stared at the husband she never felt she deserved and then at the child who was suddenly a stranger. They waited, looking back at her. She sighed. Her entire world was shattered, falling to pieces, but Tim was so strong, he sounded so confident and Marie was so small and still so much a part of her.

She slowly stepped to the car and got in. After a long hesitation, she stiffly hugged her daughter, holding her as if she were covered with diseased boils.

She sighed and said, "All right. Together we can make Marie her own person."

She just prayed that perhaps they could succeed. She smiled weakly at her family and pushed back the thoughts of smothering the child if they failed.

Reflected Glory

Dorothy Davies

Hallam Manor was everything Charles Merriman had expected it to be: an overgrown Gothic pile of stone and brick in the centre of something like – his amateur guess – 20 or so acres of finely landscaped grounds. Everything shouted money and history, the two things he wished he had and knew he was never likely to achieve. He would always be the wannabe top ranking salesman; good but not brilliant, reliable but not glittering in the eyes of his employers. Even his company car, a BMW, was not the top of the range model the higher ranking salesmen were given.

He sighed as he parked the now dusty midnight blue vehicle alongside the gleaming black and silver ones already in the parking area. No doubt their luggage was leather where his was fabric, but – he reminded himself constantly, he had been invited to this conference weekend, hadn't he? They must see something in him, surely.

He couldn't conquer the feeling of total inadequacy, though, even more so when a man in tails and white shirt – belatedly he realised this was the butler – welcomed him with a bow, took his fabric suitcase and solemnly escorted him to a room on the third floor at the far end of a long portrait lined corridor. Charles gazed around with studied indifference, but inside he was a boiling mass of anticipation, burgeoning anger, *why was he being put so far away from everyone* and outright panic that he would say the wrong thing, do the wrong thing. Did one tip a butler, for example? It had never occurred to him to find out.

Fortunately, several of his stomach-churning problems were resolved when the butler opened the door.

"Here's your room, Mr Merriman. We only allow exceptional guests to use this, it is an indication of the high regard Somantomics has for you. I am Bernard. You can ask for me by phone or send a messenger if there is something you want. And..." he held up a perfectly manicured right hand, "you don't tip butlers. If you wish to tip the messenger, waiter or anyone else, that is entirely your choice but they are all highly paid. Now, may I suggest you have a short rest, perhaps a bath or shower to help you relax? The dinner gong will be sounded at 7. You can meet your fellow associates for sherry before dinner at 7.30 sharp."

Before Charles could even blink, Bernard was gone, a silent gliding figure making his rapid way back along the corridor to the stairs. He turned around, saw the suitcase on the bed and wondered how it had got there; he hadn't seen Bernard move from the doorway whilst he had gone through what was obviously his prepared standard speech.

Even as he discarded the implied compliment about his being an exceptional guest, he knew all about corporate b.s, Charles took in the Gothic glory of the room he had for the weekend and sighed with contentment. It was everything he wanted, a huge comfortable looking bed with satin covered pillows, a table stocked with drinks and tea making equipment, desk with laptop and telephone, a huge walk in wardrobe, and 54" TV with remote just waiting for him.

He turned round, gazing at the walls; then caught sight of himself in the massive overmantel mirror. He looked ordinary, too ordinary to be in such an opulent room. All his neuroses of not being good enough crashed back in and he watched his reflected shoulders slump.

And then rise up again.

But he hadn't moved.

The image in the mirror was standing straight and tall, with a confident grin changing his face, proper confidence, not a fake put-on-for-the-customer grin.

Slowly Charles began to emulate the grin and felt his facial muscles move, but the image remained the same.

He went over to the mirror, watching the image walk toward him, exactly the same. But not entirely… there were subtle differences; he reached the fireplace before the reflection did.

"I'm over tired, long journey, best unpack, get my suit hung up, get the wrinkles out, get myself that bath Bernard talked of..."

Talking for the sake of it, talking so he wouldn't look at a mirror that didn't reflect everything as it should.

Talking so he really didn't hear the mirror say, 'that's a good idea, old man.'…did he…

Charles responded to the dinner gong by striding along the corridor, taking the stairs with careless abandon and walking confidently into the lounge, carrying a glass of sherry as if he did it every evening, not only on these social occasions. He chatted with a group of fellow employees, feeling as if he was on their level, not striving to be on their level. He caught sight of himself in the huge overmantel mirror in the lounge, a copy of the one in his room. For a moment he hesitated but this time the reflection appeared to be an exact copy.

The other one, the strangely off-centre not-quite-right one in his room had to be some kind of fluke. Perhaps it was antique, the mirror slightly mis-cast, perhaps it was put in that room away from the other more highly rated sales personnel. Perhaps…

Dinner was announced and, as one, the group moved into the dining room. For the moment, Charles' stomach's needs overtook his need to work out what was wrong about the mirror in his room, apart from the fact it showed him as he would like to be, not as he was.

About half way through the third course, Charles realised something, with a shock so profound it was a wonder half the diners hadn't seen his look of surprise.

He *was* being the person in the mirror. He had not fluffed his anecdotes, spilled any wine, dripped gravy on the immaculate snowfield that covered the table, he had not elbowed anyone; he had perfect manners and perfect aplomb.

Just like his reflection.

Am I the reflection? He asked himself the question whilst knowing it was a foolish one at best, verging on the insane at worst. How could he be his own reflection?

When the pep talk and itinerary for the weekend was over, Charles stretched, stood up and made his way over to the fireplace to study the mirror.

It looked normal. It showed the room exactly as it was and exactly how Charles was. Confident. Fluent. Articulate. A hundred other words to describe the man he had always wanted to be. In that moment he wanted nothing more than to go back up to his room and see what the mirror had to show him.

As if on cue, the group began to disperse, 'goodnight's being called, hands shaken, shoulders clasped; all the bonhomie of sophisticated men who knew their way around the commercial world, by God, let no one doubt it.

Charles went back to his room feeling as if he was walking at least twelve inches off the carpeted corridor. He had never felt like that before. It was something he thought he could get used to.

The mirror waited, patiently hanging over the fireplace as it had done for how many years? He walked over to it, noticing yet again that his reflection did not match his movements precisely; there was a fraction of time between each step, each swing of his arm, each movement of his hand as he smoothed the lines in his face.

The reflection showed someone even more confident, even more suave, even more man-about-town than Charles was at that moment. He hadn't thought it possible but he was there.

'I want to be you!' he said in a fierce whisper, wondering if he had gone entirely and completely mad, had too much wine with dinner or generally flipped out by being so assured all through a dinner which would normally have given him chronic indigestion through nerves alone.

'I don't want to be you!' said the mirror in return.

Charles straightened up. "Why not?"

"You're a weakling, a wannabe, a vassal to the others, a mere shadow of what I am and what's more-" the reflection twisted its face into a scowl of utter disapproval. "What's more, you have a conscience! How do you expect to be a high flyer in sales with a *conscience!*" It was almost an obscene word in the reflection's bitter mouth.

"What can I do…" Charles stopped himself. The whole thing was ridiculous. Here he was, arguing with a mirror, with a reflection – his reflection. It was truly insane.

"No, it isn't!" snapped the reflection. "Yes, I can read thoughts! What this commercial world needs is ruthless men, brutal men, smiling faces concealing the teeth. How else do you make a mark in this dog-eat-dog environment? Well, little weakling, what answer do you have?"

Charles thought of the assured men he had shared dinner with, thought of their discreet gold jewellery and perfectly tailored evening suits, handmade shoes and perfect dental work. He was a mere shadow to them, no matter how hard he worked, how much effort he put in on occasions like this.

"I want it." He said it with utter calm, complete assurity. "I want to be you."

"So be it."

The reflection disappeared. Charles was staring at his room, empty of people, even though he knew he still stood in front of the mirror. It was the most disconcerting thing he had ever seen.

Then a figure came slowly out of a mist, forming into a version of himself right there in the centre. A figure with slumped shoulders and turned down mouth, a figure that shouted 'loser' to the world.

The new Charles walked into the bathroom and stared at the full length mirror over the bath. He was there, all of him, the new 'him', military stance, sleekly groomed, slightly feral glint in his eyes and a hint of savagery in his grin.

"That'll do me well." He decided to go downstairs for a nightcap in the bar, perhaps a chat with other guests, perhaps an idea of how his new persona would reveal itself to them.

As he left his room, the figure in the mirror melted away into a blob of nothing which lost itself in the rich pile of the carpet.

Charles didn't hear the mirror murmur 'we just trapped ourselves another one, Satan.'

Nor would he have been concerned if he had.

Grooming

Wendy Lynn Newton

The old man's not looking so good.

Gaunt, like he's got an eating disorder, but I can see the sticky brown-green stain congealed by the side of his mouth. Lunch. Or what's left of it. Looks like pea and ham soup. Again. I know he's eating, but it's not hunger that's going to get him. Hunger would say something and he's got nothing more to say.

I spit on the edge of a tissue I snatch from the box next to his bed and grip his chin with my thumb and forefinger. The grey and white stubble prickles and glitters under the fluro light like mica on stony rock. Looks like three days' worth. Colour's not great either, now that I'm close, it's ashen over the sickly yellow pall he's been sporting for the last few weeks. And the smell! Disinfectant and yesterday's lunch in his teeth and old pyjamas and pee that's got nothing to do with the soup.

I feel the anger punching like a drunk in my gut.

They could at least clean him up. He's paying, for what? I rub his face so hard his head sways, but he doesn't blink an eye.

I don't know what I'll do when he's gone.

Four o'clock, on the dot, he says and I see the smile crack his face and reach the dead space in his eyes.

Me on the edge of the bed and him telling me the stories from the old days, before I was born, when he was a young gun and life held his cock in its hand. I collect the stories like butterflies, carefully noting their colour and wingspan before pinning them under glass. Preserving them, so the air can no longer get to them or make them fly away.

It's important for me to keep something, I tell him, but I don't finish the sentence.

When you're gone is left unsaid and I see a look that's somewhere between love and pain, because he gets it. The closer you get to the end, the smaller that distance becomes, until you realise love and pain are one in the same. Then, even goodbye doesn't need to be said.

I dip my hand into the plastic bowl, testing the water temp. Seventy degrees. I twist the buttons of his shirt singlehandedly, while the other squeezes the sponge so there's not too much water. There's a skill to it, because the nurses get shitty when they have to change wet bedsheets for nothing, but I insist on doing it. They don't argue, but I see the looks they give me when they change shift.

Between you and me, mate, I whisper and give them an imaginary finger when their backs are turned.

It's hard to believe it's the same man that smiles from the black-and-white wedding photo fading under the bedside lamp. There's barely a whisper of life left. His rotten breath rattles in his chest and his ribs poke out oddly like clothes hangers in an empty wardrobe.

Only a matter of time, the doctors say, but I'm not sure if they say it for him or for me.

His liver's shot, they say, but I know it's his heart. The heart always goes first. The heart has such mass, it can't hold itself up against the gravity that keeps pulling it down to earth. Each year goes past, dragging it closer and closer to the ground, a meteor falling through space, melting on its way down. Tiny by the time it hits but leaving a huge crater as it dies.

I wipe the sponge over his shallow, greasy chest, careful, gentle, so I don't pull on his tender skin. I can't tell if it hurts, but I'm as quick as I can be so he doesn't get cold. A quick lather up, a change of bed clothes and we're both grateful for the soapy freshness. Even the photo looks a bit brighter, like his old self is saying, *you're okay, mate, you're in good hands*.

"Tomorrow, mate?" I ask. "Four o'clock, on the dot."

But his head sinks to his chest and a thread of dribble spills down his chin.

I feel the punch of anger again. I don't know what I'll do when he's gone. *Only a matter of time*, the doctors say and I'm sure they're saying it for me.

"Ron, you're back on shift? How was the weekend?"

The RN pokes her head into the room as I tuck the sheets back into the side of the steel bed. She doesn't wait for a reply, but she's probably used to not getting one.

71

"When you're finished with Mr Brock, can you see to Mrs Harris? Her bedpan needs emptying and she could use a sponge-bath. After that, can you check with Nurse to see if the other residents need attending to? Ron? If you've got nothing else to do?"

It's not really a question. She's really saying that I'm taking too long with Mr Brock again. They all say it. But I don't care. That's my kindness. And there's so little of it left here.

I pick up Mrs Harris' bedpan, careful not to spill any of the tea-coloured piss or the tiny, black turd onto my uniform. Mrs Harris with the long silver hair and the skin that's as soft and wrinkled as century-old silk. When she sleeps, she sucks her thumb and takes shallow, irregular breaths, and if I stroke her back through the cotton flannel of her nightie, she whimpers like a baby.

I'll sprinkle her with talcum powder and wash her hair and plait it around her head, like the way she wears it in the photo by her bed. We'll share a cup of tea, sweet, like she likes it and I'll steal an extra biscuit from the kitchen so we can both enjoy a treat.

I tip the waste into the loo, flushing a couple of times to dislodge the turd and spray freshener around the room. Not looking good, that colour, I think, probably her liver, but I'll wait for the doctors to tell me it's time for her to go.

But now I've got the message loud and clear.

I can let him go tonight.

I'll ask for one more story and when the time's up I'll squeeze out the last bit of air and pin him down under that glass with his butterflies. It will be hard at first to see him go, but pain and love are one in the same. He knows that. And I'm always one to look at my cup as being half-full, not half-empty.

Mrs Harris has stories to tell. And when hers are finished, I'll press her like the dried flowers she keeps tucked in her bible and I'll move onto Mrs Cutter.

Not half full, as I think about it.

My cup is overflowing.

Love Spells Trouble

SJ Townend

I find the book I'm after under 'Hobbies' in a dusty corner and I take it to a library desk. It has a gold-leaf pentangle on the front. My index finger slides easily down the contents list, my beetle-black nail scrapes past Happiness, Health, Levitation, Prosperity and so on until . . . there it is . . . at the bottom of the list: page one hundred and six—the Love Spell.

He hasn't spoken to me—yet—but I know all about him. Everything. I think. Everything the internet and my own eyes can discover anyway. At home, in the corner of my bedroom, I've created a candle-lit shrine around a teaspoon he used last month in the canteen. Three colour photographs of his beautiful profile (which I snapped secretly and printed at work after office hours) and two nag champa joss sticks half-smouldered in one carved bone holder complete my make-shift temple to him. With the help of a little black magic, I know Frederick will be mine—Frederick and his big blue eyes, Frederick with his skin like porcelain. Skin so pale it glows bright lime green when I watch him using the photocopier as I take a little longer than I need with the industrial hole punch.

I've cast many spells before in my childhood—tossed pennies hopefully into water fountains, cast wishes before blowing out birthday cake candles, written names on pieces of paper and crumpled them under a full moon,—and sometimes, they even worked. I am now a lustful young woman. My desires have grown too great for the magic that moons and wishing wells can offer. And the spells have become more complicated.

Frederick has sat opposite me at work for months now. Never looks my way. Always seems a little miserable. I, myself, a Goth, find his moodiness quite the turn on.

I long for him to see me, to want me the way I covet him. I've never felt so passionately about anything before as I do now about him. Ever.

***

I flip to the page I need. The old library book stinks of mothballs and, oddly, my great grandmother's kitchen. There. The Love Spell, headed with a large, embellished curlicue font and a picture of two lovers entwined. Want. Need. Frederick. The spell guide tells me I need to write a letter of intention, stating what I want to happen. Oh, where shall I begin?

I want a love so strong. I want someone to embrace forever. I want us to become inseparable. I want his lips to press hard against mine. Ultimately, I want him to adore me from the moment he first sees my face once this spell has been cast and I want him to fall in love with it. I want to make him the happiest he's ever been and ever will be.

The book also states that I need him to take a sip of a love potion made from an acorn cap full of my blood stirred into the ashes of my intention letter. Acorn cap? I'm not a fucking forest sprite, I'm an office worker in a concrete city with a population of nearly eight million people. I'm biting my bottom lip as I read—it's bleeding slightly; coppery, warm, comforting. This will not be enough. I don't want to scar my face. I've a busy afternoon ahead at work unfolding and refolding paperclips and not long left to spare so I finish off scribbling down my desires on a scrap of paper, check out the book and hurry back to work. I need to bleed from somewhere else.

Back at the office, in a toilet cubicle, I drape my cardigan over the smoke detector and light the letter I've scribed. I hold it until the flames creep as close to my fingertips as I can bear, I watch the grey skin of ash which forms; a delicate layer left in the fire's wake. I tap a little of it into a pop bottle lid which I've carefully balanced on the cistern, drop the rest of the burnt letter down the toilet pan— surely I don't need it all—and flush the smoked remnants of my toasted wishes out into the sewers of the city.

Nail scissors. I take them from my handbag, slice a deep gash into my palm and squeeze until vermillion drops come. I tap off drop after drop into the bottle lid atop the heap of ash. The cap is full. The blood keeps coming. I've surely more than enough so I lick my wound clean and wrap my hand in toilet tissue. Blood leaks through like the creep of ice spreading on a lake. I unwrap my hand again, take clean tissue, and re-wrap; makeshift bandages. I wait until I feel the skin tightening underneath the tissue as my body starts preparing a fresh scab that I'll enjoy picking off later.

In my good hand, tucked under the sparkly black wool of my spider-web-stitch crochet wrist warmer, I conceal the love drug. If I'm careful, I can smuggle it back into the office like this.

One hand holds potion, the other is wrapped in crimson tissue. Nothing to see here. Perfectly normal Goth coming back from her lunch break, awkward walk, minimal eye contact. I've got this.

Frederick is at his desk, eating a tuna salad. I hate tuna. But I love Frederick so I guess I'll learn to love his fish-scented breath. Mints can do wonders. Or I can wean him onto something else. Or cast another spell, I guess. An opened can of cola sits by his mouse. I move behind him, accidentally-on-purpose brushing my hip against his shoulder. "Oh, so sorry," I say. But I'm not. For the first time ever, we make eye contact and then he speaks to me.

"What happened to your hand? Looks nasty."

He's seen me. The spell is working already and he hasn't even consumed the potion yet. Each heartbeat of mine pumps out noir confetti inside my chest. Whilst he's distracted—looking into my eyes, listening to my sweet black cherry lips—I somehow manage to tip the love drug into his drink. Stealth. Ninja moves. Goth ninja.

I feel heat in my cheeks as I spiel off some yarn about the document guillotine being hungry. Sharper than it looks. He says, "Oh," sips his drink and his eyes return to his screen. My heart is banging like a caged bird. The excitement is almost uncontainable. My happy ever after is almost tangible.

Spell complete.

He says nothing more to me, but I swear he looks in my direction sometime mid-afternoon. I think he checked me out.

***

It's Friday. Two days since I cast my spell. In my very bones, I can feel it working, ruminating. I feel like I'm walking on sunshine. Black sunshine. Birds suddenly appear every time he comes near. Ravens. You get the idea. He's mine. I can feel it.

I watch Frederick through the slim slice of soupy office air between the monitors from my side of the office. His hands are tapping on the keyboard, typing something important no doubt, he even types sexily. I wish his prim fingers were moving up and down on my flesh, caressing my skin instead of massaging QWERTY's hard grey buttons.

I notice he's wearing nail polish—I did not see that yesterday—black polish, same as mine. Snap. Meant to be. I grin at him and I see he's smiling too as he admires his own manicure. I ponder whether I should use nails as an icebreaker, see if he's into death metal too. Must be. Who isn't? But I can't bring myself to speak to him. Each time I try, my throat burns, my voice comes out funny. Words get stuck deep in my throat. Is this a side effect of love?

***

It's been six days since the spell. I'm convinced he keeps smiling at me. Or maybe it's a twitch. Either way, *he* seems a tonne happier; must be feeling something. I swear I saw him topping up the photocopier with additional paper for whoever uses it next. No-one ever does that unless they're high on drugs. Or love.

A moment ago, I dropped my stapler on the floor, so I'm on my hands and knees, grappling around in search of it amongst the industrial carpet. The carpet is burning my knees. I hope the friction isn't laddering my nylons. Where is that damn stapler? Lost, that's where; lost somewhere between the business-grey vertical vines of desk legs, cables and shadows. While crawling around on the floor, I notice Frederick is wearing my socks.

Where his slacks rise up due to his seated position, I see pink and yellow and green chequers hugging tight each of his ankles. Each sock has an image of a cartoon cat on its side. *The* Cartoon Cat. I bought them from a bespoke market stall in Holland at some point over a long weekend on the 'shrooms—they had geometric appeal.

There is *no way* he could own the same pair.

Coming back up from under the table, banging my head as I rise, I notice he's changed the top half of his outfit too. He definitely wasn't wearing *that* a moment ago. I distinctly remember he had a navy tie and a grey shirt on—I've been watching him (a tad moist-thighed) all morning from my desk, through the slit between our cuboid realms. I've even made a pencil sketch of him in said shirt and tie in my note pad. But now, he has a Nirvana t-shirt on. The one with the yellow slashed-cross dead eyes. Correction: he has *my* Nirvana t-shirt on, the one I slept in last night. Identical—same hole, same place: left sleeve. Around his neck I spot my velvet crucifix choker too.

Startled and panicked—*this is odd*—I grab my bag, push past him and the other desk slaves and leg it out of the office. I speed towards the sanctity of the toilets to splash cool water on my face. I need to snap out of this terrible hallucination. Flash backs from the summer? Have I been spiked at work? Who would do that, spike someone—at work?

I charge down the corridors, knocking into faceless others on my way and I look down at my hands. My midnight nail polish is gone. And where my black crocheted arm warmers were just moments earlier, I see grey cuffed shirt sleeves instead.

The back of each of 'my' hands is covered with a soft dusting of new, dark hair.

I push the door of the bathroom open and make it to the sink where I proceed to vomit up my eggs Benedict. I have to place my hands on the cream ceramic rim of the sink to steady myself.

As soon as my stomach is empty and I'm confident I'm in there alone, I brave looking up and into the mirror.

Big blue eyes. Wide eyes. Frederick's face staring back.

I'm in his suit. I've his trousers on. My feet are now size ten in suede brogues instead of cute purple patent t-bars.

I reach down, inside his briefs—

I scream . . . but his voice comes out instead. Clarion. Deep.

My mind, his body, his face—we've become merged, blended, inseparable.

I reach around behind me, fumbling for my handbag. I'm certain I grabbed it on my mad dash out, but instead I find a leather satchel slung over my shoulder: Frederick's leather satchel.

I pray to Mother Goddess for forgiveness, hoping I'll find the spell book I've been carrying around inside it despite my bag shifting into the shape of his. I need the book—there's *got* to be a reversal spell in it to get me out of this mess.

It's all gone terribly wrong. Yes, we've become inseparable, entwined in some bizzarro kind of way, but surely this won't make us a happy couple?

Is he sitting there, at his desk, with *my* body on as clothes? Will he wake up tomorrow with *my* face where his should be? I will never cut corners with my spells again. I'll search the entire city for a fucking acorn tree to reverse this situation, Mother Goddess, I swear. I just wanted him to fall in love with me, for him to be ecstatically happy—

Inside my/our/his bag, there's no spell book—in fact, there's nothing of mine at all.

All it contains are his belongings: tuna fucking sandwiches, mobile phone, tatty wallet, and some medical pamphlets on gender reassignment.

Of Birth - and Death

Dorothy Davies

Darkness. Total darkness.
Warmth. Surrounding warmth .
Comfort. Enshrouding comfort.
I do not wish to leave.
The voice said I have to go.
I said no.
The voice insisted.
I want to stay here in the darkness, the warmth
and the comfort.
Out there is –
Who knows?
The voice insists.
The movement begins; the movement which
will evict me.
I will not go.
The fluid carries me.
I have to go.
I will not go without retribution.
I will take with me that which enfolds me.
This sac which holds me.
That which gave me life will die with my birth.
It is only right.
I do not wish to go.
Nor does this being.
It is done…

Coming Of Age

Paul Edwards

Callum's father had always held an unhealthy fascination with the occult, and when he brought home the John Dee translated version of the *Necronomicon* – purchased from an antique bookstore located in a shadowy part of town – it signalled the end of Callum and his family.

Dad spent months studying the tome. Its archaic script looked like insects, squirming and writhing on brittle yellow pages. He quit his job so he could devote more time to his studies. Mum didn't dare complain; she was always tiptoeing around him, afraid of upsetting him in some way or another.

Sammy, Callum's sister, saw what was going on and rebelled. She ran away to live with an older boy in another part of town. Dad didn't care; his attention was focused solely on Callum, to the point where nobody else in the family mattered.

He would enter Callum's room most nights, dressed in robes and a cloak, the book laid open in his hands. He looked like some evil minister or priest, whispering and chanting at the foot of the bed. Callum would stay silent, pretending to be asleep.

One morning, while Callum was packing his bag ready for school, Dad came into his room and showed him some rare affection. He stroked

Callum's face with nicotine-stained fingers and whispered, softly, "What I'm doing is for your own good. As a father, it's my duty to prepare you. This world isn't a place for the faint-of-heart, my boy."

Dad kept up the nocturnal lessons, with Callum understanding more and more each time. He'd always feel so tired in the mornings, struggling to function and focus on school. The sermons of the *Necronomicon* weaved their magic, aging him, hardening him to the horrors of the adult world.

***

The extended family gathered for special occasions – birthdays; Christmases; bank holidays; wedding anniversaries. Dad's much more sociable brother Dom, his wife Jane and their twin sons stayed in sporadic contact. So too had Callum's great aunt, Edna. None of the extended family members were particularly close, coming together only out of mild curiosity; to compare and contrast their lives, embroiling themselves in the petty jealousies and personal conflicts that ensued, it seemed.

Before Callum's eighteenth birthday, the last family get-together was for Mum's fiftieth. Even Sammy came, bringing along with her a thirty-three-year-old bloke called Ben. Callum didn't want to ask what had happened to her previous boyfriend, the one she'd run off with.

Sammy cornered him in the kitchen, out of earshot of the other family members.

"How's it been?"

Callum shrugged. "Nothing's changed."

"It pisses me off that Mum's so submissive. Wish she'd married Uncle Dom instead. How did Dad turn out the way he is, eh?" Sammy flashed a tight, brittle smile. "If it ever gets too much, you can always come and stay with me and Ben. Right, Ben?"

Callum looked at Ben.

Ben met his gaze with a long, cold stare.

Back in the sitting room, the atmosphere changed as soon as Dad left the house to smoke a cigarette. Everyone seemed so much more relaxed and at ease.

"How've you been?" Great Aunt Edna asked Mum. "It's never too late, you know."

"Wish I could believe that."

"You *should* believe it, Angie."

"Too much has passed. I wouldn't know where to start. I'm fat and frumpy. I look in the mirror and see a stranger standing there now."

Mum glanced up, catching Callum's eye.

Confusion and sadness rippled across her features.

Pained regret, Callum sensed, that she no longer knew her own son.

***

The night before he turned eighteen, Callum was visited by his father again. He lit black candles and burned some foul-smelling incense before resuming his cruel teachings.

Callum listened to the words, not even bothering to feign sleep. He let the words steal into him, filling his essence with darkness. His mouth twisted into a grin, his gaze fastening on the shadows flickering across the walls.

The sermons were making him harder, stronger, warping him into something else completely.

His father stopped chanting suddenly.

Callum lifted his head.

"Dad?"

Candlelight washed over that cowled figure at the foot of the bed. Father was trembling, tears streaking down the length of his face.

"I'm the very worst thing in the world," he whispered.

Callum had never seen his father cry before. It sickened him deeply.

"Why have you stopped?" Callum asked. Dad looked up with a startled expression, then dropped his gaze and resumed reading.

Read and read until Callum was almost fit to burst with darkness.

***

On the afternoon of Callum's birthday, the usual suspects appeared. No one wanted to come. It was just a charade. A formality. A pathetic duty that had to be followed and adhered to.

Callum would be eighteen in five minutes' time. He felt excited and scared at the same time. He gazed about the room, half-listening to Great Aunt Edna and Mum trade stories of happier days, of better times. Uncle Dom was wrestling with his kids on the floor, Auntie Jane watching on, laughing. Sammy and Ben, who were still together, were sat at the dining table, staring out of the window at the grey, lacklustre world beyond.

Callum's gaze finally settled on Dad seated in his armchair. There was an odd expression on his father's face – something like fear, Callum thought, mingled with hope.

Dad glanced at the clock.

Two minutes to go.

He began to mutter and mumble softly, quietly, so as not to draw attention to himself.

Too late – Sammy had heard and her face flushed. "Why do you always talk to him like that?" she hissed. "You talk to him like he's a piece of shit."

Dad continued undeterred, the words squirming and scuttling their way into Callum's brain.

Callum glanced across at Sammy. "I need it," he said. "To be strong, you see."

Now everyone was looking at him.

And it was time.

Time to show them all what he was made of.

He stretched out his limbs, emitting a fierce, bestial howl. His body began to warp, twist and elongate in horrific fashion. Large, leathery spikes erupted from his back. His teeth and fingernails sprouted out, growing long and sharp, becoming weapons of grisly mass destruction.

Great Aunt Edna went hysterical, shrieking and flapping like a bird. Callum silenced her by ramming his hand into her mouth, smashing through her teeth and ripping out her tongue. The twins, screaming, leapt up and ran for the door, but Callum grabbed them both, dashing their heads together, tearing out their throats with wicked teeth and claws. He fell in front of the door, blocking the exit so that no one could escape.

Uncle Dom charged with his fists bunched and raised, but Callum was faster, stronger, ducking and dodging and sinking his fangs deep into Uncle Dom's skull. Callum tore away pieces of gristle, bone and brain as Uncle Dom toppled backwards, crashing through the wood and glass of the coffee table.

Callum spun and snatched up Auntie Jane next, her legs frantically kicking thin air. His hand clamped around her arm, ripping, tearing the limb from its socket, using it as a club to beat her with. Laughing, splashed from head to foot in blood and gore, he focused his attention next on Ben and Sammy, who were using chairs to try and break the glass of the sitting room window.

He charged them, spinning Ben around, sticking his talons straight through Ben's eyes. Ben's bloodied face struck the edge of the table as he crumpled to the ground.

Sammy sank to her knees, sobbing, pleading with Callum to let her go. Said they'd shared so much sadness and grief together, here, under this roof.

But you left me, Callum thought. *Left me here all on my own, big sister.*

His skin was literally crawling with bugs now, seeping from every orifice of his body. The words made flesh – and he was bursting with them.

He breathed in, out; in, out.

Considered Sammy for a moment.

"Cal, please…" she said.

He ripped her head clean off with one simple swipe of his claws.

A choked scream caused him to whirl, to squint, to focus on the cowering, curled-up form of his mother. He skulked toward her, grinning.

She emitted a cracked, desolate whimper. Spoke to a God she'd never had time for before.

He attacked, eviscerating her in seconds, laughing, howling, finishing off by tearing out her spine and waving it around like it was some kind of macabre trophy.

"Look at you," Dad whispered. Callum tossed the spine away and wheeled.

Dad was still in his armchair, wide-eyed, pale-faced and in awe. Something ugly and with many appendages came scuttling down Callum's body, racing across the floor and then up his father's leg.

Dad didn't even attempt to try and brush it off.

Callum half-walked, half-loped toward him, seeing brief flashes of relief behind Dad's eyes. Glimmers of realisation that he was no longer the very worst thing in the world.

Dad's mouth shaped itself into a smile.

Callum beamed malevolently back.

Then his father's limbs, flesh, and head were flying off in all different directions, a sea of blood gushing up in a gory fountain to bathe every inch of Callum's face.

He straightened at last, bloated like a balloon, flicking viscera from his claws with a black, long-forked tongue. He blinked blood, turning, gaze lasering through the glass of the gore-splattered window.

There was still so much for him to do.

The world was waiting and he couldn't wait to get out there.

To spread the hate.

Ready or not, he thought with a low, ugly snicker. *Here I come.*

Dream Catcher

Rickey Rivers Jr

An elbow in her ribs woke her up. Terrence was tossing and turning again.

"Wake up," she said.

He was struggling, shifting back and forth and turning his head from side to side. The bedsheets nearly swallowed his legs.

She gave him a shove then a harder one. He woke up, gasping. He looked around the room, and then at her. "What is it?"

"You. You're sleeping wild again."

"Oh… I'm sorry, bad dreams."

"What's going on?"

"Nothing, bad dreams."

"Okay, tell me about them."

He sat up and pushed the bedsheets from his legs. "I-uh-they're nightmares. I don't know if you want to hear them."

She sat up and turned to him. "You can tell me. We should talk about these things."

Terrence let loose a tired, half-a-laugh. "Okay, if you really want to hear it, then here goes." He exhaled, preparing himself. Telling her would hurt, he felt that. He needed time to rest his mind. He seemed to be in actual pain.

"This dream," he said. "It started a while back. It starts the same, ends the same. It starts off in a room. There's a lone baby crib and the crib is so isolated it looks like a trap."

"A baby crib trap?" she said, amused.

"I know how it sounds…" He was solemn, his mind on the dream, his eyes on a dark corner of the bedroom. "The dream," he went on, "kind of zooms in on the crib and there's a baby in there. The baby's looking up at the ceiling. It's a boy. I think it's a boy."

"You think?"

He looked at her. His eyes were tired, red and dry.

She apologized.

"No, no," he said. "I-I think the baby is supposed to be me. There's a big T on his shirt, a big blue T. So I think 'T for Terrance' right? It must be me."

"Sure," she said. She thought of other names, but kept them inside.

"But no," he went on. "A man walks into the room. The man walks up to the crib and stands over it. The room gets darker. Now the only thing visible is the baby and the man's face. The man is me. I look into the crib and I reach in. My hands move so fast."

He demonstrated. The jutting motion startled her.

He didn't notice. He went on. "My hands reach and grab for the baby's neck and I start squeezing. The baby cries or he tries to cry, but he can't get the sounds out. I'm squeezing so tight."

Her eyes widened.

"I'm still squeezing. I can feel the baby's neck crushing in my hands. His little arms move up and down. Then I'm shaking him and the head bobbles, the limbs stop moving and everything gets quiet. I drop the baby and look at my hands."

He did this now, stares at his hands. Bernice closed her eyes. In a way she wished she'd wake up too. But it wasn't a dream. She opened her eyes and saw him there. It was real. Terrence was looking down at his hands and his eyes were red and tired.

He went on. "The room fades and I hear a woman scream 'What have you done?' and then I just wake up. You know the rest. I'm sweating. I'm out of breath. I'm thrashing around. When I see that crib, every time I see it, that's when I know it'll start again. It's one of the worst nightmares I've ever had. I had nightmares as a child, but those left. This one won't leave."

She nodded.

"This one has stuck. I just want it to leave. When it restarts, I feel like screaming. I can't do anything."

Bernice was looking at him or trying her best anyway. She placed a hand on her chest. She felt pain. It hurt to see him like this. She bunched up the front of her nightgown in a vise like grip.

"I'm sorry," he said. His voice cracked. "I know, it's messed up. I don't want these dreams, but I can't stop them. They won't leave me alone."

She placed a hand on him. His skin was hot and wet. "I'm just thinking," she said. "Sometimes a dream doesn't mean anything."

He looked at her and he didn't believe her. His face gave tales of an older man.

"Or maybe they don't mean what you think they mean."

Terrence turned to the nearby lamp and clicked it on. "I know you want children. I'm not trying to… make it difficult."

She shook her head, smiling. "I know that." The smile she gave felt false even to her.

His eyes wandered. Focus left her. He wasn't thinking about the room anymore. Bernice tried to follow his gaze, but only he knew where his eyes were going. They were moving in his skull as if controlled. Once his gaze fell on her again she said his name, but he was already asking "Maybe a therapist?"

She took a moment. "Yeah, that sounds like good. We'll go together."

"That would be great. I'd like that."

"I don't want you to feel alone. We'll figure it out."

"Yeah…" He was unsure.

"Nightmares come and go. Maybe we'll get a dreamcatcher?"

"Do those things even work?"

"Maybe…" she wasn't sure. "Couldn't hurt, though."

"I guess."

"So, we'll add a therapist and a dreamcatcher to the budget."

"I'm sorry, Bern. I know we're cutting back."

"I'm joking. Don't worry. We're doing alright." She stood up from the bed and stretched. "Gotta pee, be back soon."

Bernice walked out of the bedroom. She carried her thoughts and worries with her. Terrence watched her leave. She left slow and seemed to be unbothered.

***

Terrence clicked off the lamp and put his head on the sweat soaked pillow before flipping it over and resting on the cool dry side. He felt relieved. Talking about the dream helped. It had been so hard to talk about before. He didn't expect her to take it so well, but she was always there and willing to talk even when he wasn't.

She's strong, he thought, stronger than me.

He wiped away sweat from his forehead, then his neck. Then he closed his eyes.

In the bathroom Bernice went from pacing on the cool tiles to sitting on the cool toilet seat then resting her hands on the cool sink and looking at herself in the mirror. She didn't feel cool headed.

"Tabitha, Tina, Tonya," she said these names.

"Todd, Tony, Timothy," she said these names.

Was it a premonition? She wondered. The spoken imagery of the dream came to her. It meant nothing, she knew that. Terrence was a good man, he'd never... So why was she trying to convince her reflection? She didn't know.

She recalled certain dreams did mean something. Dreams of a cat scratching had something to do with threats in reality. Dreams of drowning had something to do with being stressed, overcome. She had drowning dreams before, even falling dreams, but they didn't necessarily reflect the waking world. They were just moments your mind made up, bouts of stress trickling. She told herself this. Then she threw up.

***

After washing the vomit down the sink drain she decided to talk herself out of her own head.

"Only dreams." She said this aloud to the bathroom walls.

"Only dreams," she said this to her reflection.

Bernice left the bathroom repeating the mantra and walked out into the hallway. She stumbled a bit and caught herself on the walls. The hallway was dark, too dark. She moved along the walls toward the bedroom. It seemed further away. The dark hall seemed to play tricks, or maybe she was tired, too tired.

Finally she reached the bedroom and pushed open the door. It was pitch black. She felt the walls for the light switch but there was nothing there but wall. A smell came to her. It seemed to be vomit then she recognized the scent. She hadn't smelled an odor like that for some time, not since helping her niece with her son.

She swung her hands in front of her like swatting flies. She couldn't see her hands in the dark. She came to what felt like the middle of the room and walked directly into something waist high. It hit against her stomach. It wasn't the bed. Bernice felt around the object, the structure, an opened box. She reached inside and felt something small and warm, a child.

Bernice lifted the invisible baby and cradled it. It was real. It was warm and real and cooing. Bernice felt her heart beat for this child, her love cycle looping. Then a harsh light came dashing into the room. A man was standing in the doorway.

"Ma'am," he said. "What did you do?"

His voice was strained, like he'd been screaming for some time, screaming without notice. And Bernice went on cradling the child who was warm and so real. The man approached her and Bernice was lit up by the darkness of the outside light. She and the baby's crib seemed to glow, like they were the only two in the room full of life. Then the wall color changed from dark to white. The man was pulling her away. Bernice was screaming. The lifelike child hit the floor with no sound.

The Sea and the Statues

Paul Edwards

Harriet sat in the corner in her favourite chair.

"Sing to me, Danielle; sing to me," she said. Danielle put Drummy to bed. The clock on the wall chimed seven.

"Mummy, Drummy can't get to sleep."

"Drummy *will* sleep. Come over and sing to me." Danielle sighed and stamped her little foot before falling to Harriet's feet. She took hold of her mother's hand.

"What shall I sing to you, Mummy?"

Harriet could see Danielle, but it was different to the way Danielle actually looked. In her mind she had perfect round blue eyes and beautiful blond hair. "Anything you like."

So Danielle sang her favourite song and both voice and sea merged into one harmonious sound. Harriet felt the tears slide down her cheeks.

When Danielle had finished, she let go of her mother's hand and gazed up at her room. "I wonder if Drummy can dream. Like I can."

"Isn't he asleep yet?"

"No. He's sitting in bed listening to the sea. Mummy, do dreams come true?"

"Sometimes. What is it you dream, Danielle?"

The girl paused, then paced the room. She kept glaring up at the clock. Finally she spoke. "I dream Drummy is alive. That he can talk back to me and

98

we can play hopscotch on the beach. Mummy, do you think there are other people out there?"

"Of course there are. Someday I'm sure you'll meet somebody. What's the time?"

"Somebody *not* a statue?"

"Is it gone seven?" Harriet didn't think about the statues too much. She had grown to accept them.

"Not yet."

"I don't believe you, young lady. Come on, let's get you to bed. Drummy needs the company."

***

The morning was golden and clear. Slants of sunshine cut through the crystal panes and cast Drummy in a warm glow. The puppet sat lifeless on the cabinet, smiling at no-one in particular.

Danielle was sitting at the table stirring her cereal in the milk, staring at Drummy. She winked at him and spooned herself some food.

***

And the day grew like any other day and Danielle took her mother out across the beach. She pushed Harriet along in her wheelchair. Harriet sat, quite content, enjoying the sun's warmth on her skin and the sound of the lazy waves. She smiled.

"Is the sun bright this morning?"

Danielle looked up. . "Yes, Mummy. There isn't a single cloud in the sky!"

"Oh dear. Then you can't play your favourite game today."

"Oh wait! I *can* see one. It looks like… it looks like our house by the sea. I can see the slanting roof and if I look hard, the wind-chimes through my bedroom window.

"Once, when Mummy had her sight and you hadn't even been born, I used to lie in the fields and make pictures with the clouds…"

"Maybe you'll see again one day."

Harriet turned her head. It was the only part of her body she could move. "You're changing direction."

"I had to, Mummy. There was a statue in the way."

"A pretty statue?"

"A young boy. He's got ever such a pretty face and long locks of hair. I wonder if he ever lived. Do you think that's what happens to your body, Mummy, when you go to heaven? Does it turn into a statue?"

Harriet just laughed.

***

Just of late, the statues had been building up. New ones were appearing all the time. Each one always caught a glimpse of Danielle before Danielle caught a glimpse of them.

The wind picked up and the lazy waves began to roar. Danielle put a blanket around her mother. "Shall we go now, Mummy?"

"Yes, dear. The wind is cold and the sea is restless."

"Good. I'm missing Drummy."

A bout of melancholia momentarily hung over Harriet. It was triggered by her usual twinges of guilt. Perhaps Harriet should not have brought up the child by the sea; perhaps she could have been mingled with others. No. It would have been hard.

Danielle giggled. "That new cloud looks like a snake with its tongue poking out."

"You and your strange imagination. Come on, let's hurry. There might be a storm. How quickly the weather changes."

The child steered her mother around statues and saw the house was in sight.

Then she stopped.

There was a long pause. The wind howled, cold on Harriet's face. "What's wrong? Why have we stopped?"

"*Hush,* Mummy! In the distance I can see someone…I can see him walking about!"

"What does he look like?"

"*Shush!* He's coming closer. Oh Mummy, what shall I do?" The wind blew harder and Harriet shivered.

The stranger walked closer and he lifted his head. Danielle smiled at him. For Harriet, the period of waiting was agonizing.

Then – "*Danielle!* Who is he?"

"Oh mummy, I was wrong. It was just another statue." Her disappointment sounded close to despair. Slowly they started moving again. They made their way back to the house in total silence.

***

That afternoon Danielle played with Drummy until she got bored. Then she prepared tea, careful not to cut herself whilst chopping the vegetables, and they ate in front of the fire. When the clock chimed seven, Danielle tucked Drummy into bed and helped Harriet from her chair on to the settee. She kissed her goodnight.

"Don't forget to call if you need anything," she said.

"I won't, angel," replied Harriet.

Danielle ascended the wooden steps and lay on her bed. The window was open and the wind whistled in and stroked the wind-chimes.

She was feeling better.

"Goodnight Drummy," she said, and kissed her doll. Then she rolled over and played with the snakes in her hair until she fell asleep.

Time's Up

Liam Spinage

When I take the opportunity to recall the manifold curios hoarded by my Grandpa, one in particular is always first in my thoughts. Even to recall it now causes such shivers that I reach for a pick-me-up with trembling hands. I will tell you the tale of it, for as you will come to learn, this was no common curio, no mere mundane memento. It was a thing of such dread that, many years later, I still lay at nights, unable to sleep, listening to the rhythmic patter of rain upon the roof, too fearful to slumber, its face forever burned into my soul.

The object in question was a large floor clock which, we later understood, was purchased on the very day my grandfather was born. Too big for a shelf, it stood on the hall floor, casting a long shadow over the black and white check marble tiles. Perhaps a little ostentatious for its surroundings, it nevertheless became a talking point at every family gathering. In those early days, we thought little of it. When we were young, Grandfather would pick us up in his spindly arms and lift us to the face so that we could peer at the workings and wind it up, It was taller than he was even before he became bent with age and he would lift our small frames high above his head and get us to turn the mechanism that kept the clock ticking.

The mechanism kept it ticking. That's what he told us. As I stare at it now, its luminous face casting an eerie light over my sparse lodgings, I wonder if that was ever really the case.

Ninety years. That was the eventual span of my grandfather's life: Throughout that life he became more and more fixated on that clock, which he called his treasure and his prize and occasionally his precious. Every Sunday without fail we would visit with our parents. Every Sunday without fail, he would have us wind the clock and then sit back in his rocking chair, seemingly mesmerised by the swing of the pendulum and the rhythmic tick-tock-tick-tock which echoed throughout the house. No other timepieces were permitted in the place; he strictly forbade it. My parents pandered to that simple but disturbing whim; they found it quaint, charming even. I found it irritating. I longed to know why, but I only ever visited with my parents and whenever I came close to asking the question, worried and frantic looks were exchanged. When later we drove home, there were often harsh words. I did not know then what they were afraid of. I don't even really understand it all now.

I took the opportunity once to visit Grandpa on my own. I think I was in my mid-teens at the time and rebelling against anything I could find. He was surprised but glad to see me and ushered me through into the kitchen. While he doddered around - arranging a circle of biscuits on a plate, boiling the kettle, scrabbling for tea bags in a corner cupboard - I steeled myself to ask the question, but found it could not escape my lips. Every sound in that kitchen - the clatter of mugs, the hisses of steam from the stovetop kettle, the rustling of packets - was prompted by an ominous tick from the clock in the hall. I felt sheepish even at the rebellion of wearing my digital watch and pulled down my sleeve hastily before he turned round, embarrassed both that he might see it and at my own cowardly climb down. He looked at me in that moment and knew. He peered down through furrowed brow and bushy eyebrows and cleared his throat.

"You want to know about the clock, don't you?"

I nodded.

"You can't fool me. Your dad, he never asked. He wound that clock for me for years until your hands were big enough to turn the mechanism, Never asked why. Good kid he was to me and your gran, but incurious. Not you, eh?"

I squirmed, regretting ever coming here and sipped at my tea.

"It speaks to me, that clock. It knows me. Did you know that? When I married your gran, it knew. Chimed the moment I crossed the threshold. Twenty four straight chimes. Scared her nearly to death, but she soon laughed after. Thought it was a sign of good luck. Well, we had that, all right. For twenty four years straight, we had that."

I sat, dumbfounded, not sure what to say. I decided it was best not to say anything.

"Every tick, every tock, I know. It's all I need to listen to. It's what it wants me to listen to. It has shared in my joy; it has shared in my grief, A constant companion throughout the years. Could you ever find one so faithful? Not my wife, not my dog, not even my own children, No, The clock always comes first, And what does it ask in return, really? Just a hand to wind it once a week. That's all."

I hoped that was all it really wanted. I was imaginative at that age and did not wonder how it was that a clock might have wants and desires. I left Grandpa soon after that, with two chocolate digestives in my pocket and more questions that I knew I would never have answered.

When I grew older, we visited Grandpa less often. But when we did, I always looked at the clock as if it was a living thing, as if there was something there that was reaching out to me. Every week I still wound it at my grandpa's command, even though it scared me to do so. Its face became like a nightmare to me; luminous, ominous, still there as a parting image when I closed my eyes, haunting my daydreams and nightmares alike. I heard the ticking in my head, constant, relentless. Other noises became a torture to me. I started to fail at school; the teachers' comments charting a gradual decline in my faculties, sparking rows with my parents which only brought further pain and gloom as I receded into a world of my own.

It was a rare visit many years later on his birthday that became the turning point. We trouped up as a family as we did in my youth, the car full of cases containing all we would need to spend the night at Grandpa's house. I had accepted the invite with a mixture of trepidation and fascination. The clock had not moved; had not even stopped. It loomed long shadows over the hallway as it ever had, the strangely placed rocking chair opposite it in the hall. An evening feast was had, with as much merriment as could be mustered and we turned in for the evening.

It rang and alarmed in the dead of the night. That alarm had not sounded for many years. I had only heard it once before and knew now what it foretold. The time had come to say goodbye.

We stood round his bedside while he pleaded quietly to be taken downstairs to see his beloved clock once again. Mother and Father looked aghast but willing to comply. His life seconds were numbering, they faltered. In the hall, all I could hear was a soft and muffled chime. And then, silence.

He left it to me in his will. Father looked perplexed; Mother looked worried. I didn't want it. I had seen a glimpse of the obsession it had brought out in Grandpa. I was deadly afraid of it, but even more afraid somehow of defying his wishes.

Now it sits in the single room which I laughingly call my home. I've taken myself as far away from other people as the modern world will allow. I still hear the ticking in my head; imagine the gentle swaying of the pendulum forcing my gaze. I have opened that clock a thousand times, inspected every component, taken it apart over and over and then replaced its parts with a grim fascination. Nothing I could do would make it start again. Nothing I could do would make the ticking stop in my head. I don't know why I am so afraid of it. I don't know why it haunts me so.

It has not sounded a beat since the last day in that old house. It stopped short, never to go again when the old man died.

Meet the Authors

Ed Ahern resumed writing after forty odd years in foreign intelligence and international sales. He's had over three hundred stories and poems published so far, and six books. Ed works the other side of writing at Bewildering Stories, where he sits on the review board and manages a posse of six review editors.

https://www.twitter.com/bottomstripper

https://www.facebook.com/EdAhern73/?ref=bookmarks

https://www.instagram.com/edwardahern1860/

Diane Arrelle has more than 350 short stories published and two short story collections: Just A Drop In The Cup and Seasons On The Dark Side. She, her sane husband and insane cat live on the edge of the New Jersey (USA) Pine Barrens (home of the Jersey Devil).

www.arrellewrites.com   FaceBook: Diane Arrelle

Dorothy Davies is an editor, writer, photographer and medium. Somehow all these things come together in her seemingly crowded leisure and work life. She retired from editing for a while to run a second hand shop, the best one on the Isle of Wight, but the thrill of finding and publishing outstanding stories became too much so she started again with the Gravestone Press imprint. She still runs the shop...Her book, The Skullface Chronicles, the story of a zombie taking revenge on his dysfunctional family, is available through fiction4all.com. She has a store of short stories, some of which are finding their way into the anthologies, having not seen daylight for many a long year. She also channels books from spirit authors, notable figures from our history. These can be found on the fiction4all.site under Zadkiel Publishing.

Paul Edwards is a life-long horror fan and writes his own twisted tales in any spare time that he can grab. He has seen three collections of stories published – *Now That I've Lost You* (Screaming Dreams), *Black Mirrors* (Rainfall Books) and *Night Voices* (Demain Publishing), the latter being a joint-collection with author Frank Duffy. Paul is also a fan of role-playing games, rock music and rough Somerset cider.

Thomas   M.   Malafarina (www.ThomasMMalafarina.com) is a horror fiction author from Berks County, Pennsylvania.

To date, he has published eight horror novels *What Waits Beneath*, *Burner*, *From The Dark*, *Circle Of Blood*, *Dead Kill Book 1: The Ridge of Death*, *Dead Kill Book 2: The Ridge Of Change*, *Dead Kill Book 3: The Ridge Of War* and *Death Bringer Jones, Zombie Slayer Volume 1*. He has published seven collections of horror short stories; *Thirteen Deadly Endings*, *Ghost Shadows*, *Horror Classics*, *Undead Living*, *Malaformed Realities Vol. 1, Vol. 2, Vol. 3, Vol. 4, Vol. 5* and most recently

110

Vol. 6. Volumes 7 and *8* to be released in the near future. He has also published a book of often-strange single-panel cartoons called *Yes I Smelled It Too; Cartoons For The Slightly Off Center* and will soon publish *Yes I Smelled It 2: More Cartoons For The Slightly Off Center.* All of his books are published through Hellbender Books, an imprint of Sunbury Press.(www.Sunburypress.com).

Thomas' cartoons have also appeared in Twisted Pulp Magazine and he has published two cartoon books, "Charles" and "Charles: Remember To Dismember" through Screaming Eye Press.

In addition, Thomas' stories have appeared in more than 170 anthologies and e-magazines. Some have been produced and presented for internet podcasts and radio plays as well. He has shared anthology pages with some of the biggest names in horror fiction.

Thomas is also an artist, musician, singer and songwriter.

Marise Morland has been writing science fiction since the late Sixties and is still never short of ideas. Here, for the first time, she has written about her home town and an alternate history that very nearly happened.

Wendy Lynn Newton is an Australian fiction and non-fiction writer. She is the author of two non-fiction books and her short stories and feature articles have appeared in many key international and Australian literary and media publications. Wendy is a Full Member of the Australian Society of Authors and spent several years as a member of Write Response, a team of independent Tasmanian arts reviewers, after being selected by Arts Tasmania for an arts@work mentorship. She is currently working on a young adult science fiction trilogy and lives in northern Tasmania with two out-of-control Chihuahuas and two indifferent cats.

wendy.newton.launceston@gmail.com
Instagram: @wendynewtonlaunceston

Rickey Rivers Jr was born and raised in Alabama. He is a Best of the Net nominated writer and cancer survivor. His work has appeared in the JJ Outre Review, Stellium Literary Magazine, Fabula Argentea (among other publications).

Liam A Spinage is a former philosophy student, former archaeology educator and former police clerk who spends most of his spare time on the beach gazing up at the sky and across the sea while his imagination runs riot.

SJ Townend hopes that her stories take the reader on a journey to often a dark place and only sometimes back again.

SJ won the Secret Attic short story contest (Spring 2020), has had fiction published with Sledgehammer Lit Mag, Hash Journal, Ghost Orchid Press, Bandit Fiction, Black Hare Press, Black Petals Horror Magazine, Ellipsis Zine, Gravely Unusual, Gravestone Press, Holy Flea, Horla Horror and was long listed for the Women on Writing non-fiction contest in 2020.

She has also written and self-published two dark mystery novels, both of which are available to purchase on Amazon: (Tabitha Fox Never Knocks, Twenty-Seven and the Unkindness of Crows).

Follow her on Twitter: @SJTownend